All ~~~~~~ be reproduced,
distr ~~~~~~ eans, including
photo ~~~~~~ anical methods,
without ~~~~~~ except in the case
of b~ ~~~~~~ certain other
~~~~~~ out law.

This manuscript is a working copy and is not to be shared, published, distributed, or transmitted in any format - digital or print - without the express written consent of Moguhl Ltd.

For permissions or enquiries, please contact: Info@Moguhl.com

ISBNs:
Paperback: 978-1-9192245-1-0
Audiobook: 978-1-9192245-0-3
Library: 978-1-9192245-4-1

Author Attribution

Author:
Heath KM Groves
Primary author of The Silence We Hide. Creator of Moorside House: The Series of Silence saga and principal architect for its characters, plot and vision.

Co-Author:
Eden EM Groves
Collaborative writer whose narrative contributions, character development support, and thematic insight were instrumental throughout the manuscript.

Editor:
Ged Henderson
Responsible for the editorial refinement of the manuscript, including structural feedback, narrative clarity and line editing.

Associate Editor:
Kelly-Ann Groves
Responsible for provided structural and narrative feedback as well as regional and historical accuracy throughout development.

Creative Consultant:
Jericho M Groves
Responsible for providing imaginative input and conceptual depth throughout development.

Content Warning

This book contains scenes of graphic violence, explicit language, home invasion, and portrayals of trauma that some readers may find distressing or triggering.

Reader discretion is strongly advised.
This work is intended for mature audiences only (18 years and older).
While inspired by certain real-life settings and experiences, this is a work of fiction. Any resemblance to actual persons, living or deceased, or actual events is entirely coincidental.

The publisher and author disclaim any responsibility for reactions or interpretations. Readers who may be sensitive to such content should consider their comfort level before proceeding.

Moorside House: The Series of Silence

Welcome to Book One
The Silence We Hide, which marks the beginning of
the Series of Silence.

The Series of Silence is a crafted work that spans ten novels,
broken into three trilogies and a final book, that span three
different eras and follows three interconnected families that have
occupied the same house.

Trilogy One
The House of Overaugh (2025) - Where the Silence is Faced

Book One: The Silence We Hide
Book Two: The Silence We Share
Book Three: The Silence We Reveal

Trilogy Two
The House of Hawthorn (1940s) - Where the Silence Awakens

Book Four: The Silence We Awaken
Book Five: The Silence We Suffer
Book Six: The Silence We Bury

Trilogy Three
The House of Becker (1880s) - Where the Silence Begins

Book Seven: The Silence We Create
Book Eight: The Silence We Fight
Book Nine: The Silence We Become

Book Ten: The Dark Quarters - Where the Silence Ends

Acknowledgements

The Series of Silence is a true passion project. Ten years in the making and brought to life by a close-knit family of storytellers, dreamers and obsessive researchers.

While all characters and events in this book are entirely fictional and any resemblance to real people, living or dead, is purely coincidental, our creative process has drawn deeply from lived experiences, reflections and shared emotions. That's what makes fiction powerful.

From the start, this has been a family affair. Everyone has had a hand in shaping its voice, its mysteries, and its moments of silence. The journey has brought us closer together, and for that alone, this series has already been a success in the truest sense of the word.

Across generations, creative styles and skillsets, we've worked to build a story grounded in emotion and authenticity, with historical elements carefully interwoven to maintain accuracy where needed. But most importantly, we've done this side by side as a family unit.

Success, to us, isn't defined by charts or accolades. It's about being able to take readers on a journey, together, while proudly celebrating something we built together as a family.

We sincerely hope you enjoy reading The Series of Silence as much as we've enjoyed creating it.

The Moguhl Team

(Written by Moguhl Ltd)

THE SILENCE WE HIDE

THE HOUSE OF OVERAUGH
The Series of Silence - Book 1

Prologue

Moorside House, Altham, Lancashire

Friday, 14th March 1832 – 14:00

The first thing Hannibal Leigh Becker noticed was the quiet. Not the kind born of emptiness or neglect but the hush of something complete. After eight long years of design, construction and obsession, Moorside House stood at last. Finished, whole, and finally his.

The sun had just begun its slow descent behind the western ridge, washing the building's pale sandstone walls in warm, liquid amber. The lime mortar between the stone courses had cured perfectly, now a golden hue in the falling light. Crows wheeled beyond the orchard, the wind catching the last buds of spring. Altham was still that day, as though the entire Lancashire valley was holding its breath to admire what had risen above it.

At Hannibal's side, Mary Duncuft Becker walked slowly, her arm curled through his. She moved gently, her other hand cradling their infant daughter, Sophia, no more than two months old. Her weight was soft and warm beneath the swaddling, her eyes barely open as Mary whispered soothing nonsense to her.

Ahead of them, skipping along the edge of the newly planted formal garden, their eldest daughter Lydia darted through trimmed hedges in a flutter of ribbons and pink silk, giggling as the swallows swooped overhead.

"She'll ruin those shoes before she reaches the orchard," Mary murmured.

"She'll outgrow them in a fortnight anyway, there is no taming that girl" Hannibal replied, voice filled with pride. "Let her run."

They stood still for a moment, surveying the start of their legacy.

Moorside House was no mere country residence. It was a monument to wealth, to purpose, and to permanence.

Commissioned in 1824, the house had taken eight years of careful planning and considerable expense. Becker had spared no detail, no indulgence. The stone walls were forty-five inches thick, quarried locally, cut by hand, and set with military precision. The roof, steep and proud, was laid in heavy stone, its twin chimneys already breathing smoke from hearths newly lit.

Five spacious bedrooms were each fitted with bespoke cabinetry from Manchester. Three private studies on the third floor included one with a sweeping view of the Ribble Valley. Below were the servants' quarters, lined and heated, with brass call-bells already wired.

Beneath all that, buried deep in the cool soil, was a vaulted wine cellar with three arched chambers: one for storage, one for receiving, and one fitted for the farrier, where his tools and iron stock gleamed in neat rows against the stone.

The entrance hall stretched out twenty-four feet, with polished flagstones and twin staircases that curved like the arms of a cathedral. A wide green front door sat framed in Corinthian stone columns, above which the family crest would soon be hanging.

"I can already see the children here," Mary said softly, her gaze drifting toward Lydia as she looped around the new hedgerows. "All of them. Running. Laughing. Learning. This place... it feels safe."

Hannibal smiled faintly. "I built it to last," he said. "Stone and sweat. It will outlive all of us."

That, at least, was true.

Hannibal Leigh Becker was not a man given to indulgent sentiment but today was different. He had earned this.

From his early days as an apprentice at the calico-printing works in Reddish to eventually acquiring and expanding a chemical processing plant in Altham, Hannibal had risen from merchant stock to industrial gentry.

He now employed nearly two hundred men, many of them

from families he had known since his youth. He paid well. Demanded loyalty. Expected excellence.
And now, with Moorside complete, the Becker family would take its rightful place among the landed names of Lancashire. Behind them, the house loomed: tall, perfect, and watchful.
Mary reached out and touched the wall gently with her palm.
"It's so cold still," she whispered.

"It'll warm," Hannibal said. "It just needs us to live in it."

But the stone remained cold. Not unwelcoming, not yet, just unmoved.
They stood together for another few breaths, watching Lydia chase the last of the light across the garden paths.
Hannibal placed a hand over Mary's, just where it rested against the stone.
"She'll love it here," he said. "All of them will."

Little did Hannibal know;
that this tale would span three centuries;
through three families;
and carry three secrets;
in one house.

Act I

The Incident

Chapter One

Friday, 14th March 2025 – 20:16

The smell of freshly made pizza clung to the warm air in the kitchen. Tonight, Moorside House held the kind of silence only contentment could bring. A low hum of calm that settled between walls older than any of them.
"It smells amazing Mum," Jonah said, reaching for a slice before Natalia smacked his hand away with a wooden spoon. He grinned - that same half-crooked smile that Seth had worn at his age - and danced just out of reach with the casual athleticism of someone who knew exactly how fast he was.

At 18 years of age, over 6ft and built like he spent every spare hour at the gym - though he never did - Jonah carried the same solid frame as his father. It was the way he moved that gave him away though: calm, sure and with the easy self-possession of someone who had grown up in a house where love was constant and expectations were high.

He was already half out of his hoodie, keys dangling from one hand, trainers untied, moving with a restless energy that reminded Natalia so much of Seth when they first met that it almost hurt to look at him.

"Honestly, though, I'm starving," he added, flashing her the same quicksilver charm that Seth had once deployed in bars and briefing rooms alike.

"Then maybe you shouldn't be abandoning us," Natalia replied with a grin, nudging him with her hip. She wore her usual Friday night uniform. Soft jeans, a faded sweatshirt, hair bundled messily on top of her head. There was a softness to her, a kind of quiet efficiency, but tonight there was something lighter, a rare unwinding of the day's usual tension. "Wholemeal base, homemade sauce. You won't get that at Brendan's."

"Mum, you're the best," he said, pecking her on the cheek as he prepared to leave for his friend's house. "But we're watching a heist movie and playing on the Switch. He's got a projector now; it's like IMAX in his garage."

"At least have a slice," Seth chimed in from the doorway. He leaned against the frame, arms folded, a slight smile under the edge of his beard. Seth was still broad-shouldered, the old Army frame softened only a little by time, the quiet authority about him as natural as breathing.

He radiated a kind of careful calm, like a man who had learned long ago how to control chaos but who carried its scars quietly under the surface.

Jonah glanced at the phone in his hand. "Uber's two minutes away. Love you both, though. Enjoy the carbs. Not that Izzy needs them!"

"Oi!" came Izzy's reply from the landing, her voice ricocheting down the stairwell.

"Gluten-free, actually," Natalia muttered as Jonah dashed out, flipping the lock behind him with a practised flick. "Well, it is for me anyway."

The front door shut a second later and the house settled again. Seth crossed to the island and stole a bit of crust, earning a disapproving look. "So, I can't have any, but you can?" Natalia asked, eyebrows raised.

"That was a quality control check," he said. "For your own safety. Don't want you coming down with anything now, do we!"

Natalia smiled, watching him shoulder his way out of his coat with the same stubborn efficiency Jonah showed whenever he thought nobody was looking.

Her boys, cut from the same cloth, even if one wore his heart slightly closer to the surface.

Izzy entered, barefoot and tangled in one of Seth's old Army sweatshirts, sleeves flapping well past her hands. Sixteen years of age, she moved with the casual grace of someone utterly at home, her dark hair a tangle she hadn't bothered taming all day, and a mischievous sparkle lighting up her hazel eyes.

She sniffed the air like a cartoon character, letting the pizza fragrance snake its way towards her. "If this is another quinoa experiment, I'm ordering sushi," she said, her nose wrinkling dramatically.

"It's not," Natalia said. "It's pizza, proper pizza. Just... responsible." "Ah," Izzy said. "Responsible carbs."

They sat around the kitchen table, Izzy pulling her legs up onto the chair, arms wrapped around her knees. Natalia sliced the pizza with clinical precision, each piece perfectly even. Seth flicked through his phone, lining up the film on home cinema with the same quiet purpose he applied to everything.

"What's the movie again?" Izzy asked.

"Marvel's latest. Something about alternate timelines and a raccoon with a sword - or a gun - something like that," Seth said, chuckling under his breath. His humour, like everything about him, was understated, rarely flashy but always warmly felt.

"Sounds plausible," she replied, taking a bite. "This crust is banging, by the way."

Dinner passed the way it often did on a Friday-not rushed, not drawn out, just... right. Small laughs. An eyeroll from Izzy. Seth and Natalia exchanging glances that said more than words. The sort of normal that made you forget anything bad could ever happen.

By half nine, they were curled up in the snug. As the season started to turn an early spring rain had crept in tapping lightly against the windowpanes. Seth hit play. Natalia tucked her feet under a blanket, the same one she had knitted during the long, cold winter when they moved in, some ten years previously. Izzy grabbed a cushion and hugged it to her chest like it was a life vest.

Lydia, the family's seven-year-old black Labrador, named after her famous namesake that once resided in Moorside, plodded in and took up her usual station. She rested her greying muzzle on Natalia's knee, brown eyes fixed hopefully on the snack bowl.

The snug was a strange room, even by Moorside standards. Tucked away behind the main hallway, it was small with a low ceiling, almost womb-like. Moorside House itself was a brooding Victorian manor, set deep in the Lancashire countryside, with thick stone walls in brilliant white, towering chimneys, and ivy clinging to the rear façade like old veins.

Its windows were narrow and recessed, its stone roof heavy with nearly two hundred years of history; a house that seemed not just old, but watchful.

In the snug Seth had stripped the walls back to bare stone when they first moved in, his stubbornness and attention to detail written into every uneven slab. Now the place smelt faintly of old ash, lavender wax melts and whatever weird anti-damp paint Natalia had insisted on. It was a comforting smell - home.

"Volume check," Izzy said, stretching an arm out dramatically. "Dad, if you blast my eardrums out again, I'm suing."

"That's rich, coming from the girl who watches TikTok at jet engine volume," Seth replied, thumbing the volume down a few notches.

The Amazon preview screen flickered into life, casting a soft blue glow across the stonework. The preview images flashed superheroes, alien landscapes, and explosions bigger than any real-world disaster.

Natalia snorted softly under her breath – she'd never really 'got' the whole Marvel obsession, but she loved the ritual of it. Family night, no excuses.

It was the kind of night they would remember, long after remembering became something painful.

At 11.30, Natalia switched off the TV, Izzy yawned theatrically, dragging herself upright, still wrapped in her father's old sweatshirt.

"Night, love," Natalia said, kissing her daughter's hair, breathing in the scent of teenager-shampoo, popcorn and something indefinably Izzy.

"Night," Izzy mumbled, already halfway up the stairs.

Seth turned off the kitchen light. Natalia made sure the front door was locked, the secondary bolt sliding home with a weighty clunk.

They climbed the stairs in a loving silence that came from comfort, not distance.

And Moorside House fell still.

Outside, eyes watched them climb the stairs through the landing skylight.

Chapter Two

Saturday, 15th March 2025 – 00:24

Izzy blinked into the dark, her breath shallow under the covers. Something had shifted; not a noise exactly, but a vibration, a change in the atmosphere. It was like the house had exhaled, then forgotten to breathe back in.

She squinted at her phone. 00:24. Her throat was dry; mouth parched from popcorn salt and whispered laughs that had stretched too long into the night.
She rolled onto her side, careful not to disturb Lydia, the old lady curled tight beside her. But Lydia's ears twitched anyway, sensing movement. When Izzy sat up and kicked her legs over the side of the bed, Lydia lifted her head and gave her a half-hearted huff.

The hallway beyond the bedroom was cold and unkind in the dark. Moorside House didn't hum with night life like city places did. No late buses passing by. No shouting teenagers. Just wind moaning faintly across the chimneys and the occasional creak from the bones of the house. When Moorside settled, it really settled. Izzy stepped out and pulled her sweatshirt tighter around her frame. Jonah's door which was besides hers on the right, cracked slightly as it was half open, a blue LED glow leaked into the dark, he had clearly left his PC on like he always did. Seth was forever complaining about the energy bill and Izzy always thought he had a point.

At the far end of the hall stood her parents' room, tucked away behind an entrance alcove, with the heavy oak door always closed at night. Izzy shuddered at the thought of what those two might be getting up to. No thank you: she was not thinking about anything like that at this ungodly hour.
She crossed the hall to the bathroom, bare feet soundless against the old pine flooring.

Then everything shifted.

He stepped from the shadows like he'd been carved from it. Sudden, solid, silent. Her brain didn't even catch up until the black shape moved straight into her path.
Eyes, the only visible part of a face beneath a black balaclava, met hers. Wide, feral, empty. Was it panic, fear, alarm or anger – she really couldn't tell.
She tried to scream. She didn't get the chance.
His hand clamped around her throat like a vice, the other

hand spreading over her mouth. Her back hit the sideboard at the point of her lower lumber and her shoulder blades cracked against the plaster wall behind.
Ornaments smashed to the floor apart from the large black basalt figurine that fell with a dull thud, spinning once before coming to rest in the middle of the hallway.
He pushed in close, his whole body pressing into hers, pinning her. His breath stank-sour, stale, pungent.
He hissed a shushing sound, low and hoarse. His grip tightened.
"Don't say a fucking word you little bitch!" She was terrified.
Panic flooded her body and somewhere in the pit of her stomach, a sensation bloomed; cold and crawling… as though something in the hallway had turned its attention toward her.
She kicked. Squirmed. Her lungs screamed for air, but he kept the pressure applied.

Then, Lydia.
A noise ripped the silence open, not her usual "Give me food" bark. This was the sound of attack: aggressive, unhinged, total rage. Then another and another.
Then chaos.

Lydia launched herself, jaws clamping onto the intruder's leg. He grunted, stumbled, tried to shake her off. She held on, snarling like something born wild. And then she took vicious bites in quick succession at the same spot just above the intruder's ankle.

Izzy managed a sound; a half-choke, half-scream. As she did so the intruder forced her head to the left, as if to break her neck. But the half scream was enough.

Light flared from the end of the corridor as the alcove oak door flung open.

Natalia. Silhouetted in the hallway entrance, hair wild, eyes flashing in fury.

"What the FUCK..." She was already sprinting, closing the distance in rapid time.

She charged forwards and her foot slipped on the edge of the rug, brushing against something cold and solid on the floor. The black basalt figure, still unbroken, still watching.

And something inside her ignited.

This wasn't adrenaline. It was older than that, something she'd never felt before.

Hot. Deep. Furious. Not chaotic but focused. Wrath, pure and absolute.

Surging forward again she was no longer thinking about fighting, now she was hunting. The intruder tried to turn his head, but not fast enough. Natalia hit him like a storm; a finger right in the eye and a shoulder into his ribs.

Her arms started flailing; not wild, but sharp and purposeful. She wasn't some brawler off the street; her years in the Intelligence Corps had taught her how to handle herself and growing up on a council estate had taught her when it was time to get down and dirty. Nobody threatened her family. NOBODY.

She grabbed for Izzy and wrenched her sideways, while simultaneously using the palm of her hand to force the intruder's head up. The man stretched and stumbled backwards.

Lydia continued her canine assault, blood was now slicking the floor, and the intruder looked wildly between the dog destroying his leg and the two female banshees he was trying to simultaneously hold onto and fend off.
Izzy squirmed free and dropped to the ground, coughing, gasping...
Natalia and the man were locked together, molten fury with limbs, spit, blood and expletives piercing the air. He regained control, swinging her hard against the wall, pinning her, using his head to smash her square on the forehead. Her back to the wall, her hands clawed at his mask, trying to get at his face.
The attacker grabbed Natalia's throat with his left hand and extended his arm to give himself distance and use his superior reach advantage, He lifted his right arm, as he prepared to smash Natalia full force, square in the face. His right arm cocked back.

And then another shape in the dark appeared. Silhouetted in the entranceway.
It was Seth.

Chapter Three

Saturday, 15th March 2025 – 00:26

Seth was nineteen and a half stone and six foot one. There was no chiselled six-pack, not anymore. A loving wife, homemade meals and a comfortable life had softened the edges, but the muscle memory hadn't gone anywhere. Not where it counted.
He wasn't built to pose.
He was built to move - and mass moves mass. That phrase had followed him through every fight, every throw, every punch since he was nine years old.
He'd started with Judo as a kid, before trading the tatami mats for boxing gloves when he joined the Army. Judo wasn't on offer where he was posted, but bruises were, and fists made do.

When he left the forces, he found his way into a local kickboxing gym, and he hadn't stopped training since. Ten years, twice a week, rain or shine. He was past his prime, sure;

forty-five-year-olds don't move like twenty-two-year-olds. But experience counted. Timing. Power. Composure.

There were levels to this game and Seth was still top tier, especially when things got ugly.

In most action movies, the directors would have you believe that fights last an almost infinite amount of time, punches traded like conversations, the advantage swinging one way, then the other, all choreographed for maximum spectacle.

In real life, nothing could be further from the truth.

Violence... real violence... is short. Brutal. Decisive.

Most confrontations are over in under a minute, often less. Blink, and they're done. But in the retelling, through adrenaline, trauma, shock, those moments stretch, warped and elastic, remembered in vivid detail as though time slowed down to watch.

That's how it was for Seth.

From the second he stepped into the hallway he saw everything in perfect clarity.

Natalia, pinned against the wall.

The intruder's left hand wrapped around her throat, creating distance. His right arm cocking back, fist clenched, ready to strike her face with everything he had.

Seth didn't think. He didn't need to. There was no plan, no hesitation. Only movement. Only instinct.

By the time the intruder's brain had processed Seth's silhouette, Seth had already closed the distance.

Six paces. Less than a breath.

And then Seth threw the hardest punch he had ever thrown in his life. The perfect extended right hook with brilliant technique and absolute force.

He wasn't aiming for show. He wasn't aiming to damage.

He was aiming to kill.

The intruder still had his back to Seth when the punch landed, a brutal, full-weight swing that connected square from behind on the right cheekbone. Seth felt the impact shudder up through his arm, felt the flesh give way beneath the wool of the balaclava, felt the bones beneath crack like dried timber.

The man's face collapsed inward on contact. The orbital socket shattered. His right eye burst, a mist of ocular fluid spraying onto Natalia's cheek.

The intruder's body folded left, rebounding off the hallway wall with a hollow thud, like a crash test dummy thrown in slow motion.

He let out a sound; wet, nasal, animalistic. The kind that comes from someone whose brain has just been switched off at the mains.

But Seth wasn't done.

There was no way this little fucker was walking away. Not after what he'd done. Not after what he'd tried to do to Izzy. Not after laying hands on Natalia.

One thought. One drive. No mercy.

He grabbed the back of the intruder's collar, pulling him off his feet so that he rag-dolled backwards and slammed onto the floor, on his back, arms flailing.

The intruder tried to raise his hands. A feeble instinct,

searching for air, for defence, for something, anything, to hold on to. No chance.

Seth's bare right foot rose above waist height and slammed down like a piston. He drove his heel into the centre of the man's face, not just stomping but driving it downward with everything he had. There was a crunch. A deep, wet collapse. The body beneath him jolted, hard. Arms snapped straight. Legs kicked out and limbs spasmed violently as brain and spine short-circuited in real time.

And then stillness.

No, you fucking don't.

You don't get out of this that easily.

Seth's eyes shifted slightly left to where the statue lay on the floor. He picked it up.

It was roughly the height of a medium vase, carved from dense black basalt. The shape was simple but unsettling, a cloaked figure, featureless, its head bowed in permanent grief. The arms were folded beneath heavy robes, but where limbs should have been the statue flared out into two curved, symmetrical handles, like the guards of a ceremonial dagger. Or the grip of something older. Meaner.

The stone was matte and unpolished, just rough enough to feel like it had texture, like it could absorb more than light: something deeper. It was porous in a way that whispered of blood. Of memory. It was heavier than it looked. Heavy in a way that felt intentional.

Seth had never seen a maker's mark. No signature. No name. It had three 'slash' marks on the bottom, possibly from some kind of fine blade or scratching received through the annals of time.

It had come with the house, part of the leftover furniture that filled Moorside when they bought it; all Victorian fixtures and heavy woods, sold as a set to "maintain character".

He'd always thought the piece was creepy. Had never moved it. Never dusted it.

And somewhere, buried in the back of his mind, he'd always figured it would make one hell of a knuckle-duster if he ever needed one.

Tonight, he needed one. Tonight, he would test the theory.

He punched downward onto the now prone intruder's head. The statue drove perfectly into the facial zone and Seth swore he could feel it strike the wood floor under the man's head.

Something inside him had snapped. Not like a thread breaking; No. Like a dam giving way.

It wasn't rage. Not in the way most people knew it. This was deeper. Older. A fury without temperature. Cold. Focused. Tectonic. It didn't rise; it took over. Quietly, completely.

Seth didn't hear the screaming. Didn't register Izzy's sobs or the wet slap of Lydia's paws on blood-slicked floorboards as she snarled towards the intruder. All he could hear was breath, his own, dragged in and out of his lungs working like the bellows of a furnace.

He raised the basalt figure again.

The second blow landed with a crack, dull and deep, again the sound of stone meeting bone. This shattered what was left of the other cheekbone.

The third caved the mouth inward. Teeth and blood and fragments of face started to seep through the balaclava, which

no longer resembled a round head shape, but more of an oval rugby ball, that was getting deflated with every blow.
And still, Seth kept going.
"Zdychaj, ty skurwysynu!" he screamed, he didn't know why, he just knew that he was screaming "Die, you son of a bitch!" in Polish.
Each strike came down harder, faster. His shoulder burned. His wrist began to throb. Somewhere along the way his knuckles split open, whether from the stone or the skull, he didn't know.
The statue was no longer a tool. It was an extension of him. Each impact released something, not rage, but pressure, like he'd been holding it in for decades.
Not just tonight. Not just this man. But everything.
Every time he'd swallowed his anger.
Every time he'd smiled instead of speaking.
Every time he'd protected others and paid the price himself.
Tonight, the debt was being collected.
By the fifth blow, there was no face left. Just pulp and fragments and the faint suggestion of what had been human.
By the sixth, even that was gone.
Still, Seth didn't stop.
In total 39 blows reigned down, he couldn't stop, he didn't want to stop. Not now, not ever…
Not until Natalia screamed his name, sending it across the air. Like a gunshot.

Chapter Four

Saturday, 15th March 2025 – 00:29 – The Incident

The world had stopped moving.
Seth stood frozen, his breath coming in ragged, uneven gasps. Blood dripped from his knuckles, the majority not his own: splattering dark patterns onto the pale floorboards.
He stared down at the shape at his feet. What was once a human face now barely resembled anything recognisable. Just broken bones, torn skin and raw flesh protruding through holes in a balaclava.
The hallway was silent. Natalia stood motionless, her back pressed against the wall, face pale and vacant, eyes wide but unseeing. Izzy crouched near the banister, her body shaking uncontrollably, arms wrapped tightly around herself as if trying to hold her own bones together.

"We... we have to call the police," Izzy finally whispered. Her voice cracked and faded, disappearing into the thick silence. When neither parent responded, she tried again, panic now

rising. "Did you hear me? We need to call them. Right now!"
Seth blinked, slowly and deliberate, as if trying to awaken from a terrible nightmare. His eyes shifted to Natalia's. They shared an understanding neither wanted to admit out loud.

"Natalia?" Seth asked quietly.
Natalia shook her head slowly, as if just realising where she was. "Seth, look at him... Jesus Christ... how-how are we going to explain this?"
"It was self-defence, mum" Izzy pleaded desperately. "He attacked me. We tell them the truth. They'll understand."

"No," Natalia murmured, stepping forward, her gaze fixed on the ruined body. "No, sweetheart. They won't understand this. No jury, no judge, no-one. Not like this."
Seth crouched down, his hands trembling slightly. He searched the intruder's pockets, checking trousers, jacket lining, even the insides of the man's shoes. Nothing. No distinguishing items. Clearly, the intruder had prepared carefully before coming here.

"No wallet, no phone, no ID. Nothing," Seth muttered, looking back up at Natalia. "There's nothing to identify him. He didn't bring anything."
"Who does that?" Natalia asked, incredulously. "Who comes into someone's house carrying nothing?"
"Someone who doesn't want to be known," Seth answered softly.
Natalia nodded, her expression darkening as reality sank in.

"So maybe no-one knows he's here."

"Well, certainly no-one who would admit to knowing he had come here..."

Izzy shifted anxiously, panic seeping into her voice. "What-what are you saying? You can't be serious. We. Have. To..."

"Izzy," Natalia interrupted, forcing calmness she didn't feel. "If we call the police, they'll see what's happened. Look at him. This isn't just self-defence."

"They'll take your father, probably me too. We'd be arrested. Charged. This would be a slam-dunk, an easy collar for them. They are not your friends in situations like this, Izzy. Trust me, I know."

Seth stood, breathing deeply, his eyes scanning the hallway as if searching for answers hidden in the walls. He had worked with the police on and off for years and the scary part of Natalia's statement was that every syllable was true.

The CPS would have a field day with this. The intruder's mother would be all over the news, telling the world how wonderful and misunderstood her lovable rogue of a son was. Some new-age medical diagnosis or excuse for poor parenting would be offered to shift blame, rather than admitting their own failings.

"They'd take us all," he whispered finally. "We'd spend months, maybe years in court, and then..." His voice faded, refusing to finish the thought aloud.

Izzy let out a strangled cry. Her legs buckled beneath her and Natalia rushed forward, catching her just as she fainted.

"Oh God, Izzy!" Natalia cried, her voice cracking.

"It's shock," Seth reassured her, lowering Izzy gently to the floor. "Give her a minute."

Natalia held her daughter, gently brushing Izzy's hair from her pale face. Seth paced slowly, his mind racing.

"We don't have long," Seth said, his voice hardened with clarity. "Maybe an hour, two tops before…" He glanced at the broken figure. "Before things start to turn."

Natalia swallowed hard, understanding. "The fire pit," he continued hesitantly as if being pulled towards it. "We could burn him."

Natalia's eyes widened in horror. "Are you insane? Do you know what that would smell like? The neighbours. The smoke alone would draw attention. Not to mention the DNA footprint. Smelling human barbecue at one in the morning isn't exactly normal."

"So, what?" Seth pressed, desperation sharpening his voice. "We can't exactly bury him in the garden."

"Yes," Natalia whispered, determination strengthening her voice. "We can. But not just anywhere. It must be somewhere nobody would think to look. Ever."

Seth frowned, trying to follow. "Where?"

"You just said it, the fire pit," Natalia clarified, steadier now, conviction growing. "Not in it - underneath it. The pit's permanent. Nobody questions disturbed earth there. If we dig deep enough and rebuild the pit afterwards, no dog, no search team will ever find him. Over time he'll disappear. Bones rot. Flesh decomposes."

Seth hesitated, considering, then slowly nodded and felt strangely relieved that the fire pit was the ultimate destination. "That will work. But it's got to be deep, Nat. Really deep."

"I know," she answered softly, glancing down at her unconscious daughter. "But we have no other choice. We do this, we clean everything, and then we pretend this never happened."

Seth looked back at the bloodied basalt statue, still lying ominously on the floor.

"We can try. But forgetting isn't an option - not for any of us. We need to make sure we never tell another living soul about this. That means all of us - including Izzy."

Natalia lifted Izzy's head gently onto her lap, her eyes locked on Seth. "We don't forget. But we survive. I'll make sure she's okay."

A long silence passed between them, heavy with the weight of their decision.

"Then let's get to work," Seth finally said, his voice grim but resolute.

They moved quietly, carefully, each aware their lives were changing irreversibly with every action they took. They had made their choice, and now they had to live with it.

Moorside House had claimed another secret, one that would echo through the rest of their lives.

Chapter Five

Saturday, 15th March 2025 – 00:43

Chaos.
It wasn't loud or frantic, but a quiet, simmering madness; the kind that comes when ordinary people have been forced to do extraordinary things. The kind that settles into the bones and drives every decision from that moment onwards. Pure survival mode.

Seth stared down at his hands, caked in dark, tacky blood that wasn't his own and felt his stomach churn violently. It was real, he reminded himself. This was no nightmare, this had happened, and they were all now trapped in its consequences.
"We need bin bags," Natalia said suddenly, breaking the trance-like silence. Her voice shook slightly, betraying the carefully controlled calm she was struggling to project. "Quickly."
Izzy sat curled into herself on the landing, having just come around, pale and still trembling, eyes wide and fixed on some

invisible horror playing out before her. Seth touched her shoulder gently as he passed, desperate to provide comfort, yet knowing there was none to be found.

In the kitchen, Natalia ripped open drawers, sending loose utensils clattering. Her hands shook, fingers fumbling until she found the thick roll of heavy-duty bin bags and black duct tape-known in military circles as 'black nasty'. She stared at them for a long moment before taking them upstairs.

"These don't decompose," she said quietly, eyes shifting to Seth, who stood frozen in the doorway. The implication hung heavily between them.

"Doesn't matter," Seth replied after a pause. "We can burn them afterwards. One step at a time, Nat. We'll use them to wrap the body and get it to the pit without spilling blood everywhere, then take it all off when we chuck him in. We can burn them afterwards once the hole is filled up."
She nodded slowly, gathering the courage to move. Her movements became almost robotic as she unrolled the bags, the plastic crackling in the quiet hallway. She handed them to Seth, her eyes deliberately avoiding his.

Natalia knelt, her breath hitching at the coppery scent rising around her. She carefully wrapped one bag around the intruder's feet, working methodically upwards. Seth watched for a moment before forcing himself to join her. They worked silently, bodies moving with a grim precision born of desperation.

The hardest part came when they reached the head... or what had been the head. Natalia hesitated, nausea clear on her face, blood pooling rapidly into the plastic.

"Give me the tape," Seth murmured. She passed it without comment, hand trembling. He wrapped the black tape around the mangled mess, sealing it tightly to prevent any more blood leaking onto the floor. With every winding turn of the tape, he felt the weight of what he'd done pressing heavier upon his shoulders.

When the body was fully wrapped, Seth moved quickly towards the kitchen sink. The fluorescent lights burned his eyes, but he didn't blink. He turned on the tap, water rushing into the sink, steam billowing upwards. The water turned red almost instantly, swirling down into the pipes. He froze suddenly, the realisation hitting him like a punch in the chest.

"Natalia!" he shouted, urgency thickening his voice.

She appeared almost instantly; panic etched into every line of her face. "What? What's happened?"

"The pipes," Seth said hoarsely. "His blood, my blood... it's in the pipes now. It's all flowing into the septic tank. DNA evidence."

Natalia's eyes widened, her hands covering her mouth. "Bleach," she whispered. "Bleach kills DNA, right?"

She darted off, returning moments later with a large bottle of household bleach, splashing it generously down the sink and letting it mingle with the red-tinged water. They stood silently, watching as it spiralled away, hoping it would erase their sins.

"Wait," Seth said. "We need to use this sink for all clean-up now and THEN bleach the lot. You clean up here too, and Izzy and anything with blood on it. We should wash everything in this sink with bleach and then ensure we bleach the pipes thoroughly."

Natalia glanced at the hallway floor, streaked with trails of dark, drying blood. "We need it for the floor too. We'll have to clean everything thoroughly. I'll buy some more tomorrow, but I'll disguise it within the normal shopping. Nothing looks more suspicious than a woman buying gallons of bleach and nothing else..."

Seth agreed. "But first, the body. We need to move him before he stiffens. We can clean after he's gone. I need to dig that hole first."

"Do it," Natalia urged. "I'll stay with Izzy and bleach the ornaments down."

Seth hurried outside but took a moment to steady himself as he opened the front door, pulse hammering painfully in his temples. Cold air bit sharply at his exposed skin, sobering him instantly. He grabbed the heavy garden spade from the shed, feeling its reassuring weight in his hands. As he walked to the fire pit, his eyes adjusted to the dim moonlight.

He knew exactly where he would bury the body. The most secluded corner of their land, shielded by the tall brick wall of an old shepherd's hut on the neighbour's property and ringed by thick trees. Private, hidden, perfectly concealed from any prying eyes. He realised grimly that perhaps the fire pit had been placed there exactly for this reason.

The pit itself was little more than a blackened patch of earth and ash, evidence of countless summer evenings spent roasting marshmallows. Seth cleared away the top layer of ash, his hands trembling now with adrenaline rather than shock. He laid out a large wooden board nearby, ready to pile the dirt onto so as not to spoil the grass.

Then he began to dig.

At first, the adrenaline drove him onward, strong and purposeful. Each thrust of the spade bit deeply into the cold earth, throwing dirt onto the board in rhythmic bursts. Natalia joined him after several minutes, helping clear loose soil from the edges of the growing pit. They exchanged no words. None were necessary. They both knew what they had to do.

Soon, exhaustion and stress began to take their toll. Every time the spade struck a stubborn root or glanced off a hidden stone, Seth cursed softly. Sweat soaked his shirt despite the chill of the early morning, muscles straining painfully with every movement.

Seth drove the spade into the cold soil again, the blade echoing as it came against another tangle of root. The hole was nearly four foot deep now, earth piled high behind him, steam rising from his sweat-drenched shoulders in the chill night air. Natalia had come out to oversee the proceedings and stood nearby with a torch, her breath fogging in the beam, her eyes fixed on the pit with grim determination.

Then came a different sound.

Thunk.

Not the muffled give of root or soil.

This was hollow. Metallic.

Seth paused.

He shifted the spade slightly and struck again, gentler this time. Another clunk. Something buried. Flat. Rigid. Unnatural.

He scraped with the edge of the spade, revealing the faint outline of rusted metal. Squatting, he brushed away the dirt with his gloved hands.

A handle emerged. Then a seam. Then two corroded brass hinges. The object was rectangular, maybe two to two and a half feet long and wedged tight into the earth at a slight angle.

"Nat," he called, his voice tight.

She moved closer, crouched beside him.

"What is it?"

"Chest. Old one."

They worked together, scraping back the soil, hands slick with mud. After ten long minutes, they had uncovered enough to lift.

It was a military-green steel ammunition chest, the kind used by the Home Guard during the 1940s - long and narrow, reinforced with iron banding. The paint had flaked, but faint markings were still visible in stencilled white:

W.D. STORAGE – CLASSIFIED

The lettering was smudged by time and damp, but legible.

Seth grunted, gripping the handle. "Help me."

They heaved.

The chest resisted at first, stuck in decades of compressed soil, then shifted with a crack of roots and grit.

It came free with a wet gasp, like the earth had been holding its breath.

Seth hauled it out of the pit and onto the grass.

The lid was warped shut, its hinges fused by rust and age. A padlock hung from the front clasp, corroded beyond function. Whatever was inside hadn't been touched in a long, long time.

"Jesus," Natalia whispered. "How old is this?"

"Eighty years, maybe more."

They stood over it in silence, both breathing hard.

"We'll… we'll deal with it later," Seth said finally. "After."

Natalia didn't argue. They were already racing against the clock.

The trunk was surprisingly light once it was out of the earth.

"Feels empty" Nat suggested, Seth didn't disagree.

They dragged it to the back side of the garden and stashed it behind the stacked logs.

Seth returned to the dig and Nat resumed her post as the light bearer. His breath came in sharp, shallow pants. The hole grew slowly; six feet deep, tapering narrower as it went, just wide enough for their grim purpose.

Natalia wiped sweat from Seth's forehead with a gentle touch, her eyes filled with unspoken worry. He didn't acknowledge her, couldn't meet her gaze, but took comfort in her presence. She stayed by him until finally, after more than an hour of relentless, back-breaking work, the hole was deep enough.

Seth climbed slowly from the pit, trembling, filthy, and

utterly drained. He checked his watch: 02:16. He felt a fresh wave of urgency clawing at his chest. Time was slipping away rapidly.

He walked back towards the house, every muscle screaming in protest, his body weary beyond exhaustion. Natalia followed closely, still silent but watchful, her gaze fixed worriedly on his back.
Inside, Izzy was now curled tightly on the sofa. She stared blankly, her cheeks pale and damp from tears. Seth met her eyes briefly, seeing the confusion and terror he desperately wished he could erase.
"The hole is ready," he said simply.
Natalia nodded slowly, rising and gently kissing Izzy's forehead. "Stay here, Izzy. Don't move. We'll be back soon."
Izzy said nothing, just stared into space.
Seth turned, already mentally preparing for the next grisly step. Natalia followed, her determination matching his own. They'd come this far. They couldn't stop now.

Together, they stepped into the hallway once more, prepared to finish what they had started.

Chapter Six

Saturday, 15th March 2025 – 02:23

It was surreal, the feeling of a body wrapped in plastic, held tightly in their grasp. They carried it like a heavy rug, each step careful and hesitant, each breath laboured, fear-driven exhaustion clawing at their senses. Seth braced himself against the stair rail, his muscles burning with the effort. Yet even as they struggled, something unexpected tugged at the edge of his consciousness; the weight, or rather the lack of it.
"He's lighter than I thought," Seth muttered, halfway down the stairs. "The head weighs around five kilograms on its own, maybe more…"
Natalia grimaced and said nothing, gripping tighter to the plastic-wrapped feet. The reality of their situation was inescapable: the intruder's missing head was making their task slightly less strenuous.

Seth wished that thought hadn't crossed his mind because he would have to make sure that every piece of that head was removed from the landing floor.

They reached the bottom of the staircase, pausing briefly to adjust their grip. The hallway was shadowed, eerily quiet, as if the house itself were holding its breath, waiting for them to finish their dark business.

"Ready?" Seth asked, looking across at his wife's strained face. She nodded once, sharply, determinedly. They moved through the front door into the crisp night air. They struggled forward, shoes crunching quietly on the gravel path, Seth's arms quivering under the shifting weight.

The fire pit hole loomed ahead; its secluded position masked by the shadowy cover of trees. It struck Seth that the isolation of this corner had never felt so sinister before. The pit itself, a blackened hole in the grass, was stark in the moonlight.

Carefully, they set the body down onto the pile of freshly dug earth beside the hole. The plastic crinkled loudly in the oppressive silence. Seth's breath steamed visibly in front of him.

"Let's get him unwrapped," Natalia said.

Seth nodded, kneeling to loosen the tape around the neck. They removed the bin bags carefully, plastic peeling away to reveal blood-stained clothes. Methodically, grim-faced and silent, they stripped the intruder completely, carefully placing each piece of clothing atop the pile of soil.

Although his personal hygiene left a lot to be desired, he had no distinguishing marks, he was lithe, a full-grown man, but a young one. With each item removed, the intruder lost more humanity, more of his identity-becoming just a broken form. Nameless. Faceless.

The moment had come. They lifted the naked torso and dropped him into the hole feet first. As Seth released him, he stood back sharply, fighting down a wave of nausea as the body landed awkwardly in the conical pit.

For a dreadful moment, the corpse stuck upright, torso suspended grotesquely by stiffening arms wedged against the sides, with the shoulders only a few inches from the opening of the hole.

"It's not deep enough." Anxiety edged Seth's voice.

"We don't have time to dig deeper," Natalia replied, her voice strained. She hesitated, looking down at the macabre sight. "We need to trim him, Seth."

Seth stared at her blankly for a moment. "Trim?"

"His arms and legs," she said with forced clarity. "We cut them off, stack them beneath him. It'll fit then."

Seth closed his eyes briefly, gathering himself, pushing back the revulsion swelling within. "Bleach," he said finally, voice hollow. "We'll need bleach on everything."

Natalia nodded. "Go. Get the saw. I'll wait here. That will need to be bleached as well."

Seth turned stiffly towards the shed.

On his return, he was almost halfway back to the fire pit when he saw a shadow emerge slowly from the front door of the house. Izzy stood there, pale-faced and trembling, eyes wide with horror.

Lydia came tromping outside in her usual prancing manner, tongue waving. She gave a quick bark and the proceeded to run behind the bush at the bottom of the garden, one of her usual haunts for bowel movements.

"Izzy," Seth called softly, stepping forward quickly. "Go back inside."
"No," she said, voice barely audible, stepping closer, eyes fixed on the partially buried body in the pit. "No... you can't do this. What-what are you doing?"
Natalia reached out for her; voice straining with desperation. "Izzy, you shouldn't be here. Please, just go back inside."
Seth moved closer, trying to shield the view, but Izzy's gaze shifted to the saw in his hand. Her eyes widened further, and she doubled over abruptly, retching violently into the grass.
"Izzy," Seth pleaded desperately, dropping the saw and reaching for her. "Please, you have to understand-"
"Understand what?" she screamed back, lifting her head sharply, tears streaking her pale cheeks. "That you're cutting him up? You're both sick! This isn't right. This isn't us!"
"Sweetheart," Natalia tried again, stepping closer, reaching out gently.
"Don't touch me!" Izzy yelled, recoiling sharply, eyes blazing with anger and disgust. "You said we were good people. But this? This is insane! I want nothing to do with this!"
"TOUGH!" snapped Seth.
"This little fucker tried to harm you, he put hands on your mother, he broke in, came up stairs into our personal space. And for sorting him out we are the bad bastards? I don't fucking think so Izzy... life is not bubble-gum and wishes..."
Bewildered, his daughter turned and moved back inside the house in a slow-moving procession of shock.

"Izzy, wait!" Seth pleaded as she turned. But she ignored him, the front door slamming behind her with a force that echoed through the garden.
Natalia's voice shook. "We have to finish this. Now."
Numbly, Seth retrieved the saw from the ground, hands shaking violently. They knelt by the hole, hauling the corpse up just enough to expose one limp arm.
Seth took a shuddering breath, the first stroke of the saw feeling alien, nightmarish. The grinding noise of metal on bone made Natalia cover her ears, squeezing her eyes shut.

First one arm, then the second. The torso became lighter, manageable, allowing Seth to drag the body clear from the hole entirely. Sweat and blood mingled on his hands, making the tool slippery and difficult to grip.
He cut through each leg mechanically, systematically ignoring the revulsion building in his chest.

Finally, limbs neatly severed, they lowered each piece carefully into the hole. Natalie grabbed the large bottle of bleach and poured.
Seth took up the spade, shovelling earth back into the hole, slowly hiding away the horror beneath layers of cold, damp soil. He placed the ash carefully back on top, smoothing it out to conceal all signs of disturbance. Over the ash, they placed the clothes and bin bags, rewrapped in fresh bags, masking their grim contents. Seth then stacked logs and twigs, carefully creating an innocuous pile ready to burn.
"We'll burn it all at sunrise," he said hoarsely. "Doing it at

night would attract attention. Plus, all the clean-up items that we need to use for the landing can be put here and burnt as well. I'm going to have to light quite a few wood fires over the next couple of days."

Natalia nodded, her face still pale and drawn. They gathered themselves together, away from the dreadful pit, back towards the comforting outline of their house.

Seth's mind suddenly began to race. A new terror flooded his thoughts, washing away the brief relief he'd felt moments before. He froze in his tracks, grabbing Natalia's arm tightly.

"CCTV," he whispered urgently, eyes wide with panic. "The bloody cameras. They've been recording everything."

They stared at each other. They had overlooked the simplest, most critical detail. The cameras around their home, meant to protect them, had become silent witnesses to their darkest night.

"What do we do now?" Natalia asked finally, voice barely a whisper.

Seth swallowed hard, the full weight of their situation pressing down mercilessly upon him yet again.

"I don't know. But we need to think fast, we are on multiple clocks here... daylight's creeping in, and Jonah will be back. "We'll have till mid-afternoon to make sure we're halfway straight. You're going to have to talk to Izzy. It's awful but Jonah is innocent, and we can't involve him in any of this; Izzy will be the weakest link on that front."

"I'll talk to her." Nat confirmed.

They stood together in the shadows, their lives unravelling rapidly around them, trapped by the mistakes they had yet to fully comprehend, each new complication pulling them further from safety.

Moorside House watched silently, the night air filled with secrets that would haunt them forever.

Chapter Seven

Saturday, 15th March 2025 – 03:39

Seth stood in the kitchen doorway, staring at Natalia with a numb expression. Neither spoke, the reality of their actions pressing down on them with an unbearable weight. Eventually, Seth broke the silence.

"We need to split up," he said softly, pulling Natalia from her thoughts. "I'll handle the CCTV; you start cleaning up. The quicker we move, the better chance we have of covering ourselves."

Natalia nodded slowly, her features hollowed out by stress. "Okay. I'll start on the landing, then work my way down. Bleach everything."

"Be thorough," Seth cautioned. "Everything counts now. It may be a few days before we get everything sorted, we just do things one step as a time as we think of them."

As Seth turned towards the home office where the CCTV recordings were housed, Natalia moved upstairs. Her footsteps felt heavy, each step as if she was dragging invisible chains behind her. The landing, bathed in the dim glow of the hallway lights, awaited her, a grim reminder of the violence that had unfolded just hours earlier.

She set to work immediately, donning a pair of thick rubber gloves; beginning the slow, meticulous task of scrubbing away their nightmare. Bleach filled the air with its choking chemical aroma as Natalia wiped down every surface, every object, desperate to erase even the faintest traces of blood or memory. Her movements were mechanical, driven by necessity and urgency rather than conscious thought.

Ornaments that had stood witness to countless quiet evenings were carried carefully down to the kitchen sink, now transformed into a cleansing station. She submerged each item methodically, rinsing away the stubborn, drying blood. Then she paused suddenly; her gaze drawn to the black basalt statue lying at the edge of the sink.

She reached out hesitantly, lifting the heavy stone figure, its weight strangely comforting yet unsettling at the same time. As she began scrubbing, she felt a curious resistance; it was as though the porous stone itself fought against being cleansed. The more she scrubbed, the more crimson seemed to seep forth from its surface, as if the stone itself was bleeding, releasing something it had absorbed deeply.

Natalia's hands trembled. An unexpected, profound deep sorrow washed over here. Her throat tightened painfully, and her eyes welled with tears. For reasons she couldn't comprehend, she felt grief - real and genuine. As if the statue transferred to her the anguish that it carried inside.

She blinked, wiping tears away roughly with the back of her

gloved hand, and set the statue down abruptly. Drawing a shaky breath, she stared at it, uneasy, before forcing herself to move on. There was no time to indulge in superstition. She needed to finish... and quickly.

In the office at the back of the house, Seth knelt by the security station. Their CCTV setup was robust - a pair of Swann DVR recorders, each capable of managing eight cameras, capturing every angle of Moorside House with military precision. Both units ran in parallel, each with a thirty-day loop. Now, those thirty days felt like a damning eternity.

He unplugged the cables methodically, trying not to think too deeply about the evidence contained within. Initially, he'd planned simply to destroy them, smash the drives, and dispose of them immediately. It was the only way to ensure no forensic expert could recover footage from their platters. But as his fingers hovered over the power switch, an unsettling thought occurred to him.

How had the intruder got in?

It was a question he had to answer. Frustration and fear mixed unpleasantly in his gut as he rebooted the system, turning the monitor back on. He sank into the office chair and began methodically cycling through each camera feed, eyes straining as he carefully scanned every shadowy image, every flicker of movement.

Minutes dragged painfully into an hour, then nearly two. Yet, no matter how closely Seth looked, the footage offered no clues. He saw himself and Natalia carrying the plastic-wrapped body down towards the fire pit; the gruesome journey clear and vivid, though mercifully the treeline had obscured the grisly details of the grim sawing. He breathed out heavily, muttering a silent thanks for small mercies.

Yet the intruder himself, the catalyst for their nightmare, was entirely absent. Seth's pulse quickened, a prickling sense of unease gripping him as he cycled through again, frame by frame, from multiple angles.

Nothing.

"How is that even possible?" Seth asked himself. The intruder had seemingly materialised from nowhere, bypassing every carefully positioned camera. Was it chance, luck, or something far worse? There were blind spots, but how on earth could he have known them? Was this a professional 'hit'? Surely not…

Only one door was not covered by cameras and that was the entrance way to the granny flat at the back of the building. The house was a traditional chocolate block shape with an L-shaped extension. The old servants' quarters were in that wing.

Currently, it was a self-contained flat.

Seth walked through the house to the flat and down the stairs to the door… which was wide open.

At least that was one question answered. Lord knows how long that had been left open. Seth shut and locked it, making his way back to the office.

Shaking himself free from speculation, Seth powered the system down decisively. He disconnected both DVR units, pulling them roughly from their housing. He carried them swiftly outside to the garden shed, his movements urgent now.

Inside the shed, Seth placed the DVRs on his workbench and picked up his cordless drill. Without hesitation, he drilled through the metal casings repeatedly, the high-pitched whine cutting sharply through the silence of the early morning. He punctured each drive multiple times - once, twice, three times-twenty holes per unit. He knew data recovery teams could do wonders with damaged drives, but there were limits, even for the best. The disks were shattered. Irretrievably fragmented.

Breathing heavily, Seth examined his work, sweat running down his temples despite the chill. With satisfaction tempered by the still lingering dread, he picked up the mangled recorders and took them to the car.

He stowed them securely in the boot, ready for discreet disposal at the local tip come mid-morning. Tomorrow would also require a trip to replace the DVRs; security needed to remain consistent to avoid suspicion, but that could wait.

As Seth locked the car, he glanced back toward the house, its dark silhouette imposing against the night sky. Unease settled deeper into his chest, spreading like ink through water. The absence of the intruder from the cameras troubled him profoundly. It defied explanation, logic, reason. Seth prided himself on rational thinking, yet tonight logic felt fragile, dangerously insufficient.

Back inside, Natalia had finished cleaning down the landing, her meticulous scrubbing leaving every surface sterile, faintly smelling of bleach. She moved downstairs, exhausted, arms aching, her mind fuzzy from the fumes. Seth found her in the hallway, slumped against the wall, eyes half-lidded with fatigue.

"You, okay?" he asked softly, although he knew the answer.

She looked up at him. "Are any of us ever going to be okay again, Seth?"

He hesitated before answering truthfully, "I don't know. But we don't have a choice now. We just move forwards."

Natalia nodded slowly, her gaze drifting again towards the kitchen sink, where the black basalt figure stood silently drying. A chill passed through her. She didn't mention the statue's strange bleeding, nor the inexplicable sorrow it had induced. There were enough burdens tonight without adding fear of the inexplicable.

"Did you sort out the cameras?" she finally asked, changing the subject, needing reassurance that at least one problem had been addressed.

He nodded, jaw tight. "Destroyed. We'll dump them tomorrow. New units in by afternoon."

She drew in a shaky breath. "Good."

"We're tired, we WILL have made mistakes, we have to understand that this is a process, and we have to spend the next few days retracing our steps, actioning items… making sure we're bulletproof."

They stood in silence for a long moment, lost in their separate horrors, each haunted by what they'd seen, by what they'd done. The house wrapped itself around them, heavy and oppressive, as if silently witnessing their torment.

"We need rest," Seth eventually said, breaking the silence.

"Tomorrow won't be any easier. We'll need to talk to Izzy first thing."
Natalia nodded mutely, pushing herself away from the wall. Her limbs moved as if full of lead, every step an effort. Her eyes were hollow, but behind that hollowness sat something unsettled. Uneasy.
"I'll go and sleep in her room till the morning," she murmured. "We need to make sure she's okay."
Seth didn't reply at first. He just stared at her - really stared - like he was seeing her for the first time after everything they'd done.
Then he asked, softly, "Nat... is it just me, or did that feel... strange, not just wrong?"
Natalia looked at him, her brow furrowing slightly. "Yeah, I know what you mean..."
"I mean," he said, hesitating, "I've been in fights. I've seen blokes lose control before and I've even lost control before. But tonight? That wasn't just rage. That wasn't even me. It felt... like something else was in charge. And how swiftly and accurately we decided to dispose of the body... that's not us."
Natalia nodded slowly, eyes moist. "You were screaming on the landing. Not just shouting; screaming. Like something ancient was pouring out of you. I swear to the Lord I was going to scratch that guys face off, I wasn't even giving it a second thought!"
Seth's lips tightened. He looked down at his bloodied knuckles, flexing the fingers cautiously. "I think I was shouting 'Die you bastard' in Polish."
"In Polish?" she echoed.

"Yeah. I... I don't know how I know that. I just do. I knew what it meant as I said it. It wasn't a translation I made. It was just... there."

Natalia blinked slowly, the weight of the moment making the air feel thicker. "Seth... we both went mad. I've never attacked anyone in my life. Not like that. I didn't think. I just launched myself at him like I was possessed."

"I think you were," Seth said quietly. "And so was I."

They stood in silence for a long beat.

"I felt it," Natalia whispered, her voice cracking. "When my foot touched that statue, something surged up through me. Not adrenaline, not panic. Something deeper. Something old. I wasn't scared anymore. I wasn't even thinking. I just knew I was going to hurt him."

Seth looked toward the kitchen, toward where the statue still sat, unmoving and silent.

"There's something wrong with that thing," he said. "I always thought it was creepy, but tonight... I don't know. It felt like it was watching us."

Natalia wrapped her arms around herself. "We buried a body tonight, Seth. We scrubbed blood out of the floor. We lied to our daughter and agreed to never speak of it again. That's not us. That's not who we are."

"I know," Seth murmured. "But it happened. And I don't think it's just trauma. I think something else is going on here."

"You think we were influenced?" she asked, almost mockingly. "By what? Some haunted rock from a Victorian sideboard?"

"I don't know," he admitted. "But I know how I felt. And how I didn't feel. I should have hesitated. I should have felt horror or pity. But all I felt was... rage."

Natalia let out a shaky breath. "And sorrow. God, I felt so much sorrow."

"Yeah."

They exchanged a long look amid the sinking realisation that what had happened that night couldn't be undone or easily explained.

"I'm scared, Seth," Natalia admitted. "Not just about what we did but about what we're becoming."

Seth reached out, gently touching her hand. "We'll deal with it. Together. But I think we need to keep an eye on each other. On all of us."

Natalia nodded. "If it changes us. If we change... I want to know."

He squeezed her fingers. "Then we watch each other's backs. Always."

They stood for another moment in that strange, sterile silence before finally, silently, heading up the stairs; Natalia peeling off toward Izzy's room, Seth turning into the alcove.

Behind them, in the dim kitchen, the black basalt statue stood alone on the counter.

Still.

Dry.

And waiting, watching...

The dream came fast.

Izzy was standing in the middle of the lane that ran along the eastern edge of the Moorside estate. The road was narrow and dark, swallowed on both sides by towering hedgerows and trees that leaned inward like skeletal fingers. The sky above was bruised violet, thick with rolling clouds that moved too slowly to be natural. The wind didn't blow; it hovered, pressing the air against her skin like a warning.
Then the sound came. Bare feet slapping against damp earth. She turned.
A little girl in a white nightgown was sprinting barefoot along the outer field. The grass was tall, tangled, whispering secrets as it pulled at her legs. The girl's hair, also tangled and honey-blonde, fanned out behind her like a streamer in the wind. She was tiny. Too tiny to be alone.
Izzy felt her pulse rise.
"Hey!" she called out. But her voice vanished in the air, muffled like she was shouting underwater.
She tried to move but her feet wouldn't. Her legs locked in place. She wasn't in control here.
The girl ran faster.
Then came the scream.
"Lottie!"
It rang across the sky. Sharp, desperate, and raw. A woman's voice, breaking under the weight of fear.
"Lottie! Please come back!"
The girl didn't stop. She darted through a gap in the hedge and into the lower meadow at the base of Moorside's sloping

hill. The earth was muddy there, thick and uneven, but she barely noticed. Her arms flailed with urgency.

Izzy's gaze snapped to the house. And she felt her chest tighten.

Moorside stood on the hill above, tall and terrible in its stillness. The windows weren't just dark. They were hollow, hungry. The chimneys, like spires, warped and wrong. Ivy twisted up the walls like veins. The stone was slick, blackened as if it had been burned.

It was watching. She could feel it.

Something growled in the distance. Not a dog. Not anything alive. It was low. Inhuman.

A vehicle sat idling at the side of the house. A 1940s van, Army green with rusted doors and rotting tyres. The engine clattered in slow, unnatural rhythms. The back doors were open, revealing only blackness. It looked like a waiting mouth.

The girl slowed for just a second, hesitating near the boundary fence. Her chest rose and fell rapidly. She looked around.

And then she looked at Izzy.

Eyes wide. Unblinking. Pleading.

Izzy's breath caught. The girl looked so familiar, but she knew they'd never met.

And then the wind shifted.

From the tree line behind the girl, a figure emerged.

Tall. Rigid. Face obscured beneath a wide-brimmed hat. He wore a long black coat that moved in the wind though he made no sound. No footsteps. No breath. Just presence.

He didn't run.
He didn't need to.
He glided across the grass, like time bent around him.
The girl screamed. Not words. Just terror. A piercing, primal shriek that made Izzy's knees buckle.
"LOTTIE!" the woman's voice cried again.
It was too late.
The man lunged, moving impossibly fast, as if he had always been beside her. He tackled her into the dirt, arms locking around her middle.
Izzy screamed. Finally. Loudly. Horrified.
But no one heard.
She tried to run, to move, to get to her but the road was gone. The hedge was gone. The field had become smoke.
And the man. He turned.
Slowly. Precisely.
He looked straight at her.
His face wasn't a face. It was a blur. A depthless void. It was as if something had reached into the idea of a man and erased the details.
She couldn't breathe. Couldn't think. Her blood screamed.
Then, all at once, the sky cracked. A sharp, jagged line of white light split the clouds.
The ground twisted beneath her feet.
And Izzy woke up beside her mother, gasping for air.
The word 'Lottie' still echoing inside her skull like it had been branded there.

Chapter Eight

Saturday, 15th March 2025 – 07:46

Natalia opened her eyes slowly, consciousness creeping back painfully, reality returning in hesitant fragments. Warm daylight spilled softly across Izzy's bedroom walls, painting gentle golden patterns onto the pastel wallpaper. For a fleeting moment, she felt strangely disconnected, as if everything had been nothing more than a vivid, disturbing nightmare.

But as her memory returned, so did the dread.
Izzy stirred beside her, curled up protectively against her mother. Natalia had spent the remainder of the early hours here, hoping her presence would provide comfort. She had drifted off only briefly, sleep overtaking her despite herself.
Suddenly, Izzy jolted awake, a sharp cry escaping her lips.
"No!"
"Shhh..." Natalia murmured, tightening her gentle hold around Izzy. "It's alright, Izzy. You're safe. I'm here."
Izzy's eyes darted around the room, her chest heaving as tears

pooled and fell freely onto her pillow. The thoughts of the little girl were quickly replaced with the events of the evening.
"Mum... It-it really happened, didn't it?"
Natalia hesitated, then nodded gently. "Yes, sweetheart, it did."
Izzy's face crumple. "How can we live like this? Knowing what we did... what Dad did? How can we pretend?"

Natalia's reply was quiet but firm, carrying a conviction born from sheer necessity. "Because we must, Izzy. The world isn't as black and white as it seems. People think life is simple - that good and bad are easy to separate. But reality... reality is far messier."

Izzy's eyes met her mother's, searching for answers, pleading for comfort. "I don't know if I can live with it, mum."
"You can," Natalia responded reassuringly, her fingers smoothing her daughter's hair. "We have no choice. And Jonah - he's innocent. Completely. We need to protect him, Izzy. Whatever it costs us, we cannot let him suffer."
Izzy closed her eyes, her breathing still shaky and uneven. "But why us, mum? Why our family? Why did this happen to us?"
Natalia's voice softened further, her tone almost broken. "Sometimes, terrible things happen, and there's no explanation, Izzy. We can't control that. All we can control is how we respond, how we survive.
"It might not feel right, but we're doing what we must. It's a cross your father and I must bear. Not you, not Jonah."

"I don't think it's that simple," Izzy said sadly. "I don't think you can just hide from it. It's everywhere. It's in the walls; it's in the air. It's never going away."

Natalia reached out, gently cupping Izzy's tear-stained face. "You're right, love. It isn't going away. But it will get easier to carry. Eventually."

Izzy took a deep, trembling breath, clearly struggling with the heaviness of her mother's words. Natalia gently kissed her forehead, then drew back, offering a weary smile.

"You should rest," she suggested softly. "Stay in bed. Try to sleep a bit more. Later this afternoon, we can go for a walk. Get out of this house for a while."

Izzy nodded slowly, clearly exhausted beyond words, yet grateful for the small mercy of a moments escape. Natalia remained beside her, trying to restore some tiny measure of comfort.

They sat quietly, the silence between them disrupted only by the distant sound of footsteps approaching from the hallway. Seth stood at the doorway, his shoulders sagging under an invisible burden. His voice was low. "Izzy... Natalia... I-I'm so sorry. I wish there had been another way, I really do. But there wasn't."

Izzy looked up at him. Despite the anger and pain of the previous night, she recognised something equally broken in her father's face. Something genuine.

"I know, dad," she told him eventually. "I know."

Seth crossed the room cautiously, kneeling beside the bed. Natalia reached out for him instinctively, pulling him close, their bodies leaning together, their shared grief like a living force between them. Izzy shifted slightly, allowing herself to be drawn into the embrace.

They held each other quietly, tears silently tracing paths down their faces, grief mingling with mutual comfort. No words were needed; no apologies or explanations could lessen the pain. Yet, being together made it bearable. Just.

Izzy's voice broke the silence, soft yet sharp with anguish. "This silence... it hurts. It's unbearable."

Seth raised his head slowly, meeting his daughter's gaze with quiet understanding, his voice soft yet full of conviction. "Yes, Izzy. But this is the silence we hide."

Izzy closed her eyes again, her breath catching softly at her father's words. The phrase hung between them, perfectly capturing the raw truth they now faced.

The three of them sat. Their silence no longer a burden carried alone, but a pain acknowledged and borne together.

Chapter Nine

Saturday, 15th March 2025 – 08:56

Morning sunlight filtered through the kitchen windows, its soft warmth seeming to mock the grim undertones that filled the air. Seth stood at the foot of the stairs, waiting patiently as Natalia and Izzy emerged from the bedroom, their expressions haunted by the sleepless night.
"Morning," Seth muttered awkwardly, noting their dishevelled appearances. His gaze moved between Natalia's pale face and Izzy's wary eyes, both still shadowed by the lingering fear of last night's horror. "I hate to ask you both this, but... I need all the clothes you were wearing. Everything."
Natalia hesitated, her fingers unconsciously clutching at the hem of her pyjama top. She exchanged a look with Izzy, understanding passing silently between them.
"Of course," Natalia finally responded, her voice strained yet steady. "Give us a second."
Seth waited quietly, gaze lowered, listening to the soft rustle

of fabric and muffled footsteps above. Moments later, they returned to the landing, Natalia handing over a tightly bundled collection of clothes. Seth took them carefully, placing each item meticulously into a large black bin bag he'd retrieved from the kitchen earlier.
Izzy shifted uncomfortably. "Is that everything? Will it really help?"
Seth nodded grimly. "Yes. It must. The smallest thing could leave evidence. It all goes in the fire."
Natalia swallowed. "I'll start breakfast. Pancakes, something light."
Seth waited until Natalia and Izzy headed downstairs to the kitchen then he turned and stepped outside, bin bags in hand.

The morning air hit him abruptly, refreshing yet sobering, as he crossed the damp grass to the fire pit. The evidence lay waiting beneath the carefully stacked wood and ash. Bleached and gruesome memories that needed obliteration. Seth knelt and arranged the bags carefully, tucking them deep within the logs and kindling he'd prepared the night before.

He returned to the garage, locating the small green petrol canister which he carried carefully back to the pit. With precision born from anxious necessity, he poured just enough petrol onto the stacked wood and bags to guarantee ignition. Stepping back, Seth paused briefly, the smell of petrol sharp in his nostrils, before striking a match. It flickered briefly between his fingers before he tossed it gently onto the pile.

The fire ignited instantly, flames leaping hungrily, consuming the bags and clothing. Seth stood, watching the bright orange glow and twisting smoke.

"This isn't enough. Not nearly enough," he told himself.

He knew he would need more fires to erase every fragment, every possible trace that could link them back to the intruder. This was only the beginning.

Seth remained at the fire's edge a little longer, ensuring everything burned evenly, before finally turning towards the house. As he moved across the grass, a car slowed at the driveway entrance - a dark grey Uber pulling to a halt.

Jonah stepped out, tousled hair sticking up in every direction, his expression faintly sheepish when he spotted his father.

"Morning, Jonah," Seth called out, forcing casual warmth into his voice, masking the strain beneath.

Jonah flinched, clearly startled. "Oh-hey Dad. Didn't expect to see you out here."

"Clearly," Seth said drily, a half-smile touching his lips. "What happened? Wet the bed?"

Jonah stared blankly for a moment, clearly not understanding. "Wait-what?"

Seth chuckled, though the sound felt oddly foreign. Forced. "You're home early, mate. Usually, people your age only surface this early if they've had an accident and had to rush home."

Jonah rolled his eyes dramatically, shaking his head. "Hilarious, dad. Truly."

He moved past to avoid further scrutiny. Seth watched his son's back, unsure if Jonah had sensed the tension in the air, or if his mood was simply typical teenage reluctance.

Jonah stepped into the kitchen, instantly pulling a face. "God, what's that smell? It reeks of bleach in here!"
Natalia glanced up from the stove, attempting a casual expression despite the alarm ringing loudly in her chest. "Little mishap cleaning up earlier. Nothing serious."
Izzy's voice came dryly from the table, her expression neutral. "Yeah, Mum and I decided to reinvent our hair care routine. Bleach is apparently great for volume."
Jonah stared at them both, clearly unconvinced, before shaking his head in confusion. "You two look like you've been dragged through a bush backwards. Seriously, what the hell happened to you both?"
Natalia forced a tight smile, flipping a pancake carefully in the pan. "Late night. Your sister and I didn't get much sleep."
Jonah shrugged, apparently losing interest. "Whatever. I'm gonna go shower and crash. Don't burn breakfast."

He jogged upstairs, unaware of the tension that lingered behind him.
Natalia turned sharply; eyes wide as she glanced toward Izzy. "That was close," she whispered tensely. "We need to be careful."
Izzy, leaning back casually in her chair, raised an eyebrow at her mother. "Come on, Mum, don't lose your head. Jonah's as dumb as a post."

Natalia's jaw tightened, her eyes instantly flashing with sharp rebuke. Seth had stepped into the kitchen just in time to hear Izzy's remark, his expression darkening noticeably.

Izzy caught their simultaneous sharp looks and shrugged, a defiant, nervous edge creeping into her voice. "Oh, what? Too soon?"

Seth exhaled slowly, frustration battling with exhaustion on his face. "Izzy, joking is one thing but now is really not the time. Please."

Izzy lowered her eyes, mumbling softly. "Yeah right…"

The tension lingered. Seth moved towards the table, sinking heavily into one of the chairs, his gaze drifting thoughtfully out the kitchen window toward the fire pit, still gently smoking in the distance.

Natalia placed a plate of pancakes gently onto the table, her movements slow and careful, trying to restore a faint sense of normality.

"We have to be more careful around Jonah," she said finally, softly. "We can't afford to slip up."

Seth nodded slowly, meeting her worried eyes. "Agreed. From now on, everything we do, everything we say, must seem perfectly normal. Especially around him."

Izzy picked up a pancake, pushing syrup around her plate. "He wouldn't believe it anyway," she muttered. "He trusts us."

Natalia, her voice gentle but firm, replied. "Exactly why we can't betray that trust. We're protecting him - keeping him safe. None of this touches him, Izzy."

Seth reached out, gently taking Natalia's hand across the table. "We've already taken care of the most dangerous part. As long as we stay careful, stick together, we'll be alright."

Natalia smiled faintly, though worry still clouded her eyes. "I just want it over. I just want everything back to normal."

Seth nodded, squeezing her hand gently. "It will be. Eventually."

They sat quietly around the table, the silence heavy yet somehow comforting - a quiet agreement between them that survival depended upon secrecy, carefulness, and an unspoken unity. Beyond the window, the fire slowly burned itself out, evidence reduced to ash and smoke.

But the real weight - the burden of guilt, secrecy, and fear - remained firmly upon their shoulders, an unseen shadow trailing closely behind, invisible but always present.

Chapter Ten

Saturday, 15th March 2025 – 10:32

Seth pulled on his coat and reached for his car keys. He felt exhausted, the fatigue not just physical, but deeply embedded in his bones. There was so much still to do, so many loose ends, and each task seemed heavier than the last.
As he stepped out the door, Jonah's voice startled him from above, echoing down from an open window.
"Hey, Dad! Where are you heading?"
Seth looked up, trying to suppress his irritation and anxiety. He forced a casual smile, masking his inner dread. "Just heading to Costco. Need to replace the DVRs."
"Mind if I tag along?" Jonah called down. Seth hesitated but he knew refusal would only raise suspicion. He swallowed hard, "Sure. I'll wait in the car."
He watched Jonah vanish from the window, his stomach knotting tightly. "Fuck," he uttered under his breath, quickly opening the boot of his car to glance at the damaged DVRs - two units peppered with drill holes, thoroughly destroyed.

Jonah emerged from the house, pulling on his hoodie and climbing into the passenger seat beside his father, cheerful and oblivious. "Ready when you are," Jonah announced, distractedly checking his phone.

They drove quietly towards Whinney Hill tip first, silence filling the vehicle. Jonah's eyes narrowed slightly as Seth parked by the skips, pulling out the mangled DVRs and tossing them unceremoniously into the electronics disposal bin.
"Dad, those DVRs looked wrecked," Jonah observed, lifting an eyebrow.

Seth laughed lightly, attempting to sound casual. "You can never be too careful destroying hard drives, Jonah. Better safe than sorry. Anyway, I'm switching us over to those cloud-based Ping cameras. Much better image quality, more secure."
Jonah nodded slowly, not fully paying attention, eyes fixed on his phone. "Sure, whatever you think best."
The Costco store was busy, crowded aisles buzzing with Saturday shoppers. Seth moved purposefully, pulling out a trolley, while Jonah wandered behind him distractedly, eyes continually flicking to his phone. Seth glanced back at him, irritated yet grateful that Jonah wasn't paying close attention to what they were buying.

He quickly located the new Ping camera system; cloud-based, wireless, easier to control remotely and far less suspicious. He placed the camera system into the trolley, along with several other unrelated items: biscuits, cakes, steaks, and a few bottles of wine, hoping to make the shopping appear as casual and innocent as possible.

Near the checkout, a small UV flashlight caught Seth's eye. He reached for it, feeling slightly guilty, yet grateful for its usefulness. It would help tremendously, he thought, a way to double-check everything - carpets, walls, hallways, every inch. Jonah looked up from his phone long enough to observe the flashlight, frowning slightly. "Why do you need a UV torch, Dad? Planning on solving a crime?"
Seth forced a smile, nerves jangling. "Very funny. Thought it might help me check around the pipes and bathroom for leaks. They glow under UV light."
Jonah shrugged disinterestedly, clearly not invested in the explanation.
At the checkout, Seth paid quickly, got his receipt scribbled by the member of staff at the exit and loaded the shopping into the car. Jonah trailing silently behind.

On the drive home, Jonah announced casually, "I'll stay home tonight. Been a while since I've had tea with you guys on a Saturday."
Seth smiled faintly. "We're honoured by your presence, Jonah."

While Seth was away, Natalia had spent time restoring the ornaments to their places around the house, each item painstakingly cleaned, disinfected, and replaced. But one item continued to draw her attention. The black basalt statue. She lifted it again, feeling its familiar weight in her hands. It felt strangely warm, almost alive. She knew rationally it was simply stone, yet an inexplicable pull drew her to examine it closer.

Izzy wandered over, noticing her mother's intense focus. "What is it Mum?"

Natalia shook her head, confused. "I don't know. I just can't throw this away. It feels wrong."

Izzy hesitated, reaching out to touch the statue briefly. "I feel it too. I can't explain why, but it… it should stay."

Natalia turned it over, inspecting it carefully. Her heart skipped when she noticed three long, fine cuts etched into its base. They were faint, but clearly deliberate. Razor-like scratches, hectic yet oddly precise, purposeful.

She ran a finger gently over the cuts, eyes narrowing thoughtfully. "These weren't this deep before."

Izzy joined her in rubbing her fingers over the lines, briefly their fingertips touched…

"…Lottie…"

Natalia shook her head. "Did you hear that?"

Izzy spun and said: "What... Lottie?"

"Yeah…" They both looked at each other in confusion.

Lydia came bounding up the stairs and broke the moment. Natalia put the statue back on the sideboard and before she could dwell any further, a small spatter of dried blood on the radiator caught her eye.

Muttering softly, Natalia grabbed a cloth and bleach, returning immediately to scrub away the stubborn stain, her hands trembling slightly.

Seth and Jonah arrived home shortly after, Jonah quickly vanishing upstairs to his room, still engrossed in his phone. Seth set the shopping down carefully on the kitchen counter, exhaling deeply as he met Natalia's gaze.

"I bought a UV light," he said quietly. "We can check everything."

Seth hesitated briefly, lowering his voice further. "Jonah's staying in tonight, so let's wait until he's at college on Monday."

"Great idea", Natalia's phone buzzed on the counter with a varied bunch of missed correspondences, This time the screen lite up with a familiar name.

Jane Hughes.

Two missed calls already. She sighed and pressed the screen dark with her thumb. She couldn't be doing with Jane right now - the endless questions, the nosy tone wrapped up as "concern." Nat found her tiresome at the best of times, and tonight wasn't even close to that.

She shoved the phone back under a stack of post and went back to scrubbing the worktop, knuckles white around the cloth.

The rest of Saturday passed in strained silence. The family moved around each other, each distracted, lost in their own

thoughts. Lydia sensed the tension, whining softly, pacing restlessly, as unsettled as the rest of them.
They spent the evening in the snug trying to act normal, before everyone peeled off to bed simultaneously.

Nat and Seth slumped into bed, too tired to even contemplate discussing the events of the weekend.
Natalia wondered how she would ever sleep normally again… and then... darkness...

The dream came fast.

She was standing at the edge of the long, sloping field that curled like a ribbon in front of Moorside House. The sky above was iron-grey, thick with a stillness that felt wrong. The wind moved through the tall grass in long, mournful waves, carrying the low, endless hum of something ancient and unsettled.

A little girl in a white nightgown ran barefoot through the grass, her feet barely brushing the ground. Her arms pumped at her sides, hair flying like golden silk in the dim light. She couldn't have been more than eight. Fragile. Frightened.
Natalia tried to move. To call out. But her body was frozen. She couldn't reach the child. Couldn't even whisper her name.
The girl ran with the panicked grace of someone who knew she was being hunted.
And then she heard it.
"Lottie!"
A woman's voice, distant and raw. Not the comforting cry of a mother calling a child to safety, but something more frantic. Grief-laced. Terrified.
"Lottie, please!"
The girl didn't slow. She ran harder.
Natalia's eyes darted to the house.
Moorside stood silently in the distance, unchanged and yet utterly wrong. Its stone was younger somehow, cleaner, sharper, like it had been newly painted. The windows were pitch black. Ominous. Watching. The whole house seemed

to lean toward the field, as though straining to reach the girl. Then her gaze shifted.

A battered 1940s box van sat parked by the house, military green, paint peeling. Its back doors hung open. Smoke chuffed weakly from the tailpipe. Something about it felt wrong, misplaced. Like it had been waiting there too long. Like it belonged to someone who had never left.

The girl stumbled, catching her foot on something hidden beneath the grass. She hit the earth hard, but scrambled back up immediately, glancing over her shoulder.

For the first time, Natalia saw her face.

Pale. Dirt on her cheek. Eyes wide with terror.

And recognition, the girl knew she was being watched.

Natalia's breath caught in her throat.

And then from the tree line. Movement.

A figure.

He didn't run. He emerged.

Male. Tall. Thin but purposeful. His coat was long, dark wool that flared slightly at the hem. A hat shadowed his face, but Natalia saw the wrongness in him immediately. The jagged edges of his silhouette. The unnatural stillness in his gait.

He didn't run like a person. He glided.

The girl screamed.

"LOTTIE!"

The voice again. More urgent. More broken.

And then he was on her.

The man lunged, cutting across the field like wind through fire. The girl barely turned before he slammed into her, arms around her middle, crushing her into the dirt. The scream stopped short.

Natalia tried to move. To scream. To run.

She couldn't.

All she could do was watch as the man pinned the child to the ground.

And then he turned.

Slowly. Deliberately.

Though his face was still veiled in shadow, Natalia felt the pull of it. That eyeless stare. A consciousness that shouldn't exist.

And for a moment, she knew - not thought, not guessed - she knew that the girl was real.

The field began to twist. The trees convulsed. The sky cracked.

And Natalia woke up.

Sweating. Heart pounding.

The name Lottie still echoing in her ears.

Monday morning Jonah left early, oblivious to the heavy mood hanging over the household. Natalia waited until Seth had also headed out, finally picking up the UV flashlight.

She closed the curtains in the hallway and switched it on hesitantly, the ultraviolet glow washing eerily over the hall. Slowly, methodically, she moved around the room, crawling along the carpet, scanning carefully, her heart pounding uncomfortably fast.

Small glowing flecks appeared, spots she'd missed. Natalia scrubbed them quickly, fiercely, bleach-soaked cloth biting her skin. Yet with every spot cleaned, more seemed to emerge, mocking her relentless efforts with smearing ease.

She paused for a moment, breathing heavily, the reality of her situation fully hitting her. Who even were they anymore? A respectable family reduced to crawling through their home with a UV light, scrubbing away evidence of violence. This wasn't them. This couldn't be. What was happening?

She rested back on her knees, the flashlight heavy in her hand. For a brief, terrible instant, Natalia felt completely untethered, adrift in a new reality that no longer made sense.

"What have we become?" she whispered, her voice shaking with exhaustion.

There was no answer. Only silence, thick and oppressive, reminding her that there was no turning back, no undoing the past.

She steadied herself. The only choice left was to survive, no matter how grim the means or how twisted the path. Natalia closed her eyes briefly, regaining her composure before continuing her task, accepting this was now who they had to be. The statue watched in silence.

Chapter Eleven

Friday, 21st March 2025 – 19:42

A week passed slowly, marked by cautious movements and strained normality. Seth had maintained his nightly ritual meticulously; lighting fires at dusk, ensuring each night that the flames consumed evidence piece by piece, inch by inch. The fire pit became a familiar fixture once again, its nightly blaze no longer alarming to Jonah, who accepted his father's newfound enthusiasm for burning garden rubbish with a disinterested shrug.

At first, the ritual had unnerved Natalia and Izzy, the sight of the flames a constant reminder of that terrible night. But as days went by without incident, a fragile calm began to settle over Moorside house. They could almost believe, at moments, that their lives had resumed to something close to normal. Lydia, too, seemed to sense the return of stability; she became less anxious, less prone to pacing restlessly through rooms, her tail wagging cautiously as if gauging the emotional climate.

Life drifted into a cautious, deliberate rhythm. Jonah, preoccupied with his phone, hardly registered the subtle tension that lingered within the walls of their home. As far as he knew, nothing had changed beyond his father's sudden inclination for regular incineration.

Natalia found solace in routine, embracing mundane tasks as if they could erase the stain of violence. She cleaned obsessively, moving from room to room, ensuring each corner was spotless, each ornament meticulously polished.

Yet despite her best efforts, each day ended with the unsettling thought that something remained unfinished, unresolved, still haunting the edges of their lives.

Izzy, on the other hand, retreated inwardly, spending long hours in her bedroom, sketching quietly or staring blankly out of the window. The statue seemed to increasingly fascinate her, drawing her gaze repeatedly, almost as though it silently whispered secrets that only she could hear. Though Izzy never spoke openly about these feelings, Natalia noticed her frequent lingering near the object. Natalia herself felt its strange pull, unable to part with it, despite knowing instinctively she should. And so, seven days later, on the following Friday, the family found themselves once again gathered in the kitchen, preparing their weekly pizza ritual. Natalia stood at the counter, flour-dusted fingers working dough into a neat circle, spreading tomato sauce carefully across its surface. The routine felt comforting, a gesture toward normalcy that eased the constant tension, at least for tonight. Seth busied himself by slicing vegetables, his movements practiced and calm, his face betraying none of the anxiety he felt inside. Jonah lounged carelessly at the table, thumbing through his phone, occasionally glancing up to make teasing remarks.

"Careful there, Mum," Jonah joked, eyeing Natalia's precise attention to her task. "That pizza looks like it's heading towards perfection territory."

Natalia gave him a wry smile, playfully waving the wooden spoon in his direction like always. "And since when is perfection a crime?"

"Just feels suspiciously like effort," Jonah shot back, grinning. Izzy smiled faintly, her mood lightening momentarily as Lydia wagged her tail hopefully beside the oven, clearly anticipating dropped toppings or accidental generosity.

The pizzas emerged golden and bubbling from the oven, their warm aroma filling the kitchen. They ate quickly, their conversation deliberately casual, topics carefully safe and trivial. Seth felt himself relaxing slightly, grateful for the fragile veneer. After dinner, they moved quietly into the snug, a familiar routine repeated from the previous week. Lydia followed eagerly, settling herself comfortably near Izzy's feet, sighing contentedly as she nestled into the thick carpet. The snug's warm glow provided comforting sanctuary, a cocoon against the darkness outside. The TV flickered to life.

"What's tonight's cinematic masterpiece, then?" Jonah asked, settling comfortably into the corner sofa, stretching lazily.

"Something involving a car chase and explosions, if I'm not mistaken," Seth replied dryly, flicking through the streaming options.

"Ah," Jonah nodded sagely. "Highbrow cultural enrichment,

as always." Izzy rolled her eyes, smiling. "As if you'd have it any other way."

A gentle laughter rippled around the room, quiet yet genuine, momentarily dissolving their individual anxieties. Seth allowed himself to relax fully into the moment, feeling an unexpected surge of hope that they might eventually put all this behind them.

Then, abruptly, the peace shattered.

Lydia raised her head sharply, ears pricking attentively. A low growl rumbled deep in her chest. Izzy glanced nervously towards the window, instantly alert. "What's wrong, girl?"

The room fell silent, tense anticipation replacing comfort. A shadow moved outside, quickly followed by the crunch of gravel under car tyres. Seth stiffened, his breath hitching involuntarily in his throat. They all froze, eyes darting nervously toward the thin line of blinds covering the snug's front window.

A bright flash of blue suddenly illuminated the edge of the blinds, strobing rhythmically, casting an eerie pulse into the darkened room. Lydia barked sharply, rising to her feet protectively beside Izzy.

Jonah's face turned pale, eyes widening. "What's that?"

Seth moved to the window, pulling the blinds apart, peering outside. His heart sank instantly. Parked at the edge of their driveway was an unmarked police car, its hidden blue lights from behind the grill cutting sharply through the darkness, piercing the fragile illusion of their regained normality.

"What the hell?" Jonah whispered anxiously, standing abruptly, he was pale, drip white.

Natalia's hand trembled slightly as she touched Seth's shoulder, leaning close to look out as well. "Do you think...?"
"I don't know," Seth murmured, carefully hiding his alarm from Jonah. "Maybe it's nothing. Let's not jump to conclusions."
Jonah stared quizzically "What conclusions? About what?" his tone was almost defensive.
Izzy remained silent, her face taut with anxiety, gaze fixed fearfully on the pulsing blue glow outside. Lydia continued her quiet, uneasy growling, sensing the shift in mood.
The sharp rap of knuckles against the front door echoed through the house. Jonah moved instinctively, but Seth held up a calming hand, steadying him.
"Stay here," Seth said firmly, his tone calm but authoritative. "Let me see what's happening."
He walked quickly through the hallway, pulse hammering in his ears. The presence of police was suddenly tangible, terrifying. He opened the door slowly, greeting the officers standing rigidly on the doorstep, their faces solemn yet unreadable. Both wore grey suits of an nondescript sort, one male, one female.
"Mr. Overaugh?" the lead officer asked neutrally.
Seth swallowed hard and then nodded carefully, forcing his voice to remain steady. "Yes, officer. Can I help you?"
The male officer glanced briefly at a notebook in his hand, then fixed his eyes firmly back on Seth. "Is your son, Jonah Overaugh, at home this evening?"
Seth's heart clenched painfully in his chest, an icy wave of dread spreading through his veins. "Err yes - he's here. What's

going on?"

The second officer, younger, with a less hardened face, stepped forward slightly, her voice calm yet authoritative. "We need to speak with him regarding an ongoing missing person enquiry."

Seth frowned, confusion mingling quickly with the escalating panic inside him. "Missing person enquiry? What are you talking about? Who's missing?"

The lead officer cleared his throat, his tone remaining formal and detached. "We're investigating the disappearance of Brendan Hughes. Your son was reportedly the last known person to see him last Saturday morning. Brendan hasn't been home since, Jonah confirmed it via a phone call last Sunday when he spoke to Detective Constable McIntyre."

"Last Sunday? Phone call?" Seth spluttered.

The blonde officer nodded, clearly this was DC McIntyre.

Seth's mind reeled. Brendan Hughes, Jonah's friend. Seth had entirely forgotten about him in the chaos of the past week. A sickening realisation settled heavily in his gut, a fresh surge of anxiety tightening around his throat.

He stepped back involuntarily, gripping the door frame. "I don't understand. Brendan's missing? And you think Jonah knows something about it?"

The younger officer offered a cautious nod, sympathetic eyes briefly softening the blow of her words. "We're just trying to piece things together, Mr. Overaugh. It's routine questioning, nothing to panic about, but it is urgent. Brendan's family is very concerned. Your son's cooperation could be critical."

Seth inhaled deeply, trying to calm himself. "Of course. I'll...

I'll get him for you. Wait here, please."

He closed the door gently, turning back toward the snug where the family waited anxiously. Jonah had already risen to his feet, clearly sensing the tension radiating from his father's face.

"Dad?" Jonah asked warily. "What's going on? What do they want?"

Seth met Jonah's anxious gaze, forcing himself to remain calm. "It's the police. They want to ask you some questions about Brendan. They said they spoke to you on the phone last Sunday."

Jonah's eyes widened, fear and alarm crossing his features. "Brendan? Why?"

Natalia and Izzy stood quickly; anxiety etched clearly on their faces. Lydia, sensing the tension, began to whine softly, pacing anxiously. Seth shook his head slowly, voice low but firm. "Apparently, Brendan hasn't been home since last Friday. You were the last person known to see him."

Jonah's face paled. "That's impossible. I left his house last Saturday morning. He was fine then. I saw his Mum, I said goodbye to her as I left."

Natalia stepped forward, her voice trembling slightly as she glanced at Seth. "Maybe it's a mistake. Maybe there's been a misunderstanding."

Seth's jaw tightened. "Maybe. But the police want to speak with Jonah. They say it's urgent."

Jonah looked from his father to his mother, eyes wide and frightened. "The station? They want me to go to the police station. I haven't done anything wrong!"

Seth placed a half reassuring hand on his son's shoulder, steadying him. "We know that, Jonah. But you have to talk to them. We'll get this cleared up."

Jonah nodded weakly, visibly shaken. "Okay... okay... Fine. Let's just go."

"I'm coming with you," Seth stated firmly, his tone brokering no argument.

He led Jonah quickly back to the front door, Natalia and Izzy following anxiously behind. The officers had remained patiently on the doorstep.

"He's here," Seth announced steadily. "Jonah is ready to come with you but I'm coming as well."

The lead officer inclined his head politely. "That's fine, Mr. Overaugh. I'm Detective Sergeant Mark Hargreaves by the way. You can accompany your son to the station, but you must be in different vehicles. You can bring your own, we have parking. But we do need to speak to Jonah privately at the station first."

Jonah's eyes flashed with anxiety, his voice shaking slightly. "Privately? Why?"

"It's standard procedure," DC McIntyre explained calmly. "We need Jonah's account without influence or distraction. You'll be nearby at all times Mr Overaugh. We assure you it's routine."

Seth exchanged a tense glance with Natalia, silently acknowledging the necessity despite their fears. "Alright. Let's go." Jonah hesitated briefly before stepping forward, following the officers down the driveway towards their patrol car. Seth followed closely behind, every step feeling heavy.

Natalia stood frozen at the doorway, Izzy close beside her, both watching silently. Lydia sat quietly at their feet, once again whining softly, sensing the family's distress but unable to comfort them.

The doors of the police car closed, its headlights cutting harshly through the dark as it pulled away swiftly, leaving Natalia and Izzy standing in the chilling silence.

"What's happening, Mum?" Izzy asked, her voice breaking slightly. "This isn't about us, right? It can't be."

Natalia placed an arm around Izzy, pulling her close. "I don't know sweetheart. He hasn't done anything."

"But we have" Izzy retorted.

Even as the words left Izzy's mouth, a cold dread settled deep within Natalia. A new danger had surfaced, unanticipated and frighteningly beyond their control, threatening to unravel the fragile security they'd worked so desperately to reconstruct. Inside the police car, Jonah stared blankly out of the window, his reflection ghostly and pale against the glass. Seth sat rigidly in his own car waiting for them to set off, his mind desperately seeking explanations, solutions, anything that could clear Jonah of suspicion. Please Lord, do not let this be true.

The secret they were desperately protecting now felt sharper, heavier, more dangerous than ever.

They had survived the intrusion but now faced something potentially even more devastating; an investigation that could lead scrutiny straight back to them.

In that moment, he silently vowed they would survive this. Whatever the cost.

Act II

The Inquisition

Chapter Twelve

Friday, 21st March 2025 – 20:32

The unmarked police car pulled up to the rear entrance of the East Lancashire Custody Centre in Blackburn.
Detective Sergeant Mark Hargreaves was the first to exit. He was thickset and broad across the shoulders. Years of stress had etched deep lines into his face, and his weathered hands carried the quiet authority of someone who had spent too long documenting the aftermath of other people's worst decisions. His greying stubble shadowed a square jaw, and his eyes grey, steady, missed nothing. He adjusted his collar with the brisk efficiency of a man always halfway between paperwork and a pub fight.
Detective Constable Sarah McIntyre gave a curt nod. "On it." She opened Jonah's door gently, not roughly, not kindly just professionally. "Come on, lad. Let's get you inside."
DC Sarah McIntyre was lean and composed, with sharp cheekbones and a tightly knotted ponytail that seemed immune to the chaos of a shift.

Her expression rarely betrayed emotion. What she lacked in size, she made up for in clarity - every movement efficient, every word deliberate. There was no bluff in her tone, no soft edges to her presence; McIntyre had the quiet force of someone who had learned early that command didn't need volume, it needed certainty.

Jonah stepped out into the cold night air. He followed as instructed, glancing at Seth's car that had just arrived before the door closed again.

Seth caught a final glimpse of his son's frightened eyes before the car's tinted window turned to a black mirror.

The smell inside the station was industrial antiseptic mixed with coffee and disinfectant over institutional carpet. The desk at the far end was manned by a square-shouldered, grey-haired man wearing a stab vest and yet another world-weary expression.

This was Custody Sergeant Trevor Mallinson, a man who had spent thirty years in uniform and was utterly unmoved by panic, privilege, or tears.

The Custody Sergeant was not the highest-ranking person in the building, but they held a unique position of specific legal authority and independence where detainees were concerned. Among other things their roles included maintaining legal compliance with PACE (Police and Criminal Evidence Act 1984) and the aura of this burden radiated from Trevor Mallinson's presence.

"Evening, Trev," Hargreaves greeted him with a nod, sliding the paperwork across the desk. "We've got one for interview under caution linked to a missing person case of Brendan Hughes. Eighteen. This is Jonah Overaugh. No priors. No flight risk. He's the last known person to see Brendan. Brought him in voluntary; he's been cooperative."

Sergeant Mallinson peered at Jonah over his glasses and then turned to McIntyre. "Search him?"

"Already done. No items seized," McIntyre replied crisply, tapping her notes on her phone. "He's been quiet. Nervous but respectful, here's his wallet litter…"

Mallinson gave Jonah a long, appraising look before returning to the form on the terminal. "Any known vulnerabilities?"

"None declared. Eighteen, competent, healthy. No meds. Spoke clearly throughout," Hargreaves confirmed.

"Solicitor requested?"

"Duty," McIntyre replied. "Though we suspect they'll regret that soon enough."

As if summoned by the mention, the side door creaked open and in shuffled a man who looked like he'd been dragged backwards through a pub hedge, then forward through a filing cabinet.

Stephen Cartwright, freelance solicitor, formerly of Cartwright & Hale Solicitors in Preston, now working mostly duty shifts and clinging to relevance with a coffee-stained tie and a cracked briefcase.

"Evening," Cartwright mumbled, glancing around until he spotted Jonah. "Cartwright. Duty solicitor. Here for

Overaugh."

Mallinson raised an eyebrow, clearly unimpressed. "Cutting it close, Steve."

Cartwright waved a dismissive hand, already rummaging in his bag. "Had a call-out in Burnley. Traffic was murder."

McIntyre shot Hargreaves a knowing look. Hargreaves didn't smile.

Jonah glanced up, assessing the man who would now supposedly defend him. Cartwright looked tired, dishevelled, and already halfway through a sigh. Seth had entered the building and was watching from just outside the glass barrier. He felt his stomach sink, that dumpy sack of a man was now responsible for his son's wellbeing.

"You'll be booked in, then you'll have a private consultation with me," Mallinson said, fixing Jonah with a steady gaze. "Interview will follow. Be honest. Stay calm. It's not an arrest, it's an investigation. Understand?"

Jonah nodded faintly. "Err... Yeah."

"We'll use the small interview room tonight. McIntyre, get the paperwork ready. Cartwright, try and stay awake, will you?"

Cartwright grunted noncommittally, already loosening his collar.

From the corridor, Seth could only watch as his son was led further into the system, past a wall of posters about rights, process, and procedural fairness. It all felt sterile. Mechanical. Jonah turned once and caught Seth's eye again through the glass before vanishing from view.

They led Jonah through to the consultation room to the duty nurse and then moved out into the interview corridor and into the small staff kitchen next to the records room, a chance to regroup before things progressed.

Hargreaves leaned against the chipped counter, fingers tapping absently on a Styrofoam coffee cup. "Well," he muttered, glancing toward the glass panel that looked back onto the custody block, "that could've gone worse."

McIntyre didn't reply immediately. She pulled her hair back into a loose knot, clearly still turning things over in her head. "He was quiet," she said at last. "Too quiet. Not the cocky type. But not panicked either. Just... I don't know... guarded."

Hargreaves nodded slowly, eyes narrowing. "He's a smart kid. But his father, Seth. He looked absolutely rattled."

"Terrified," McIntyre agreed. "Genuinely like he'd just watched his whole world collapse. But not in a 'what's happening to my son' way. It was... different."

"Sketchy," Hargreaves said bluntly.

"Sketchy," she echoed.

Hargreaves sipped the coffee and grimaced. "You saw his hands? The white-knuckle grip. He wasn't just worried. That was fear. Pure fear. Like we'd caught them both red-handed."

"Except Jonah doesn't seem like he knows what we're even looking for," McIntyre said. "And if he is hiding something, he's playing it close to the chest. No eye contact. No aggression. But that long pause when I mentioned Brendan's mum, he blinked like we'd hit a nerve."

Hargreaves looked out through the narrow window at the

darkened car park beyond. "You know the gut feeling, Mac? That deep itch just behind the ribs?"

"Yeah."

"I've got it. Something's not right in that house. Family seems perfect from the outside, big place, polished image. But the way the dad watched him being led in? That wasn't just parental concern. That was someone who knows we're asking the wrong questions and is praying we don't stumble into the right ones."

McIntyre crossed her arms. "You think they're involved?"

"Maybe not directly. But he's not telling us everything. And I'd bet good money he's hiding something he doesn't want us to find."

A brief silence settled between them.

"We'll find out," McIntyre said eventually, quiet but certain. "They always crack. It's just a matter of who breaks first. The kid or the dad."

"Yeah, but we have to find a reason to question the dad first."

"True that."

Hargreaves finally dumped the coffee into the sink, the brown liquid swirling down the drain. "Let's make sure we're watching when it happens."

Outside the custody suite Cartwright, the solicitor appeared beside Seth with a sigh, like a man getting ready for a battle he didn't want. "They'll look after him. The process will play out, Mr Overaugh. It's out of our hands now and I'll do whatever I can."

But it didn't feel like that. It felt very much like it was in someone's hands and Seth had no idea whose.

Chapter Thirteen

Friday, 21st March 2025 – 21:45

The room was small, square, and stifling under the humming ceiling light. A video camera mounted in the corner blinked red. Jonah sat on one side of the table; his arms tight against his body. To his right sat Stephen Cartwright, already loosening his tie and fumbling for a pen. Across from them, DS Hargreaves and DC McIntyre sat poised, folders open, expressions neutral.
"Right," Hargreaves began, his voice slow and clear. "This is a voluntary interview under caution. The date is Friday, the twenty-first of March, twenty twenty-five. The time is 21:45 hours. The location is Interview Room 3, East Lancashire Custody Centre. Present are Detective Sergeant Mark Hargreaves, badge 0411; Detective Constable Sarah McIntyre, badge 1915; the interviewee, Jonah Overaugh; and his duty solicitor, Mr Stephen Cartwright. This interview is being audio and video recorded."
He clicked a small button on the table recorder. The device

beeped, then settled into a steady red glow.

"Jonah," Hargreaves said, folding his hands in front of him. "Do you understand why you are here?"

Jonah cleared his throat. "Yeah. You said Brendan Hughes. He's missing."

"That's right," McIntyre said. "And you were the last confirmed person to see him, is that correct?"

Jonah shifted. "Not sure, I guess so. If that's what you're saying"

Hargreaves leaned forward slightly. "Let's start with last Friday night. Where were you?"

"We were at Brendan's place," Jonah replied. "All night."

"Was that in his garage?"

"Yeah. We were playing on the Switch."

"Just the two of you?"

"Yeah."

McIntyre scribbled something in her notebook. Hargreaves didn't blink.

"No one else came by?"

"No."

"Did you leave at any point during the night?"

"No."

"What time did you leave Brendan's house the next morning?"

"About nine."

Hargreaves flipped a page. "And did you see Brendan's family members at all?"

"Yeah. His mum, she was in the kitchen. I said goodbye to her."

McIntyre's pen paused for a moment. "Thank you, Jonah, we've already spoken to Brendan's mum. She says she said goodbye to you, but Brendan was nowhere to be seen."
Jonah's mouth opened, then shut.
"He was still in bed"
"Really?"
Cartwright leaned in. "You're under no obligation to respond to that. Just stay calm."
"Did you have your phone with you?"
"Yes"
"All night?"
"Yes"
"Did Brendan have his phone?"
"Yes"
"You saw him with it did you?"
"Yeah, he's always on it."
Hargreaves tapped his folder. "Jonah, you and Brendan stayed in all night, is that what you are saying?"
"Yes – you can check our phone records if you like"
"Oh, don't worry, we already have." Hargreaves tapped his folder harder.
Jonah's mouth quivered again and the shut.
McIntyre cut across the silence "Do you drive Jonah?"
"N-No" Jonah stammered.
"No, you've not passed your test or no you can't drive?"
"Well, I'm taking lessons."
"How close are you to passing your test?"
"I have a booking for next week."
"So, it's safe to say you can operate a motor vehicle, just not

legally"

"Well, yeah... I suppose..."

"You suppose?" Mcintyre let the statement hang in the air, leaving Jonah to stew in his own thoughts.

Cartwright seemed to be doodling on his pad. Jonah could see squiggles. Cartwright sensed eyes on him and spluttered "Err is this going anywhere?"

Hargreaves didn't even glance in his direction.

"Does Brendan have a car, Jonah?"

"Yeah, A Hyundai i10..."

"What colour?"

"White"

"Is this Brendan's car Jonah?" Hargreaves opened his folder half an inch and took out the first of what looked like many photographs. It was a picture from Brendan's Instagram, showing him beaming next to his new pride and joy.

"Yeah" Joanah said.

"Have you ever driven his car, Jonah?"

"No."

"Are you absolutely sure?"

"Yes."

McIntyre moved her finger towards to the recorder.

"This interview is being suspended at 21:58 hours for a short break. All present remain the same. Recording will be resumed shortly."

Hargreaves and McIntyre, stood up in unison and both walked towards the door in short order.

Jonah looked at Cartwright, Cartwright just shrugged.
They stepped out of the interview room and let the door close behind them. The moment it shut; Hargreaves' mask dropped.
He turned sharply to McIntyre, voice low and clipped. "He's pissing down our legs and calling it rain."
McIntyre folded her arms. "He's lying through his teeth. That whole thing about the Switch? No activity. Nothing. Not even a bloody screen flicker from the router logs."
Hargreaves ran a hand through his hair. "You see the way he flinched when I tapped the folder? He's sitting on something. And I'm telling you, I reckon dad knows too. That man looked like he was braced for a fucking execution."
McIntyre stepped in closer. "So, what's the move?"
He didn't hesitate. "We go back in and bleed him. No more softly, softly. Hit him with everything and get this wrapped up."
"And if he still doesn't talk?"
"Then we charge him with perverting the course of justice and hold him on suspicion of involvement in Brendan's disappearance."
McIntyre raised an eyebrow. "Are we charging him tonight?"
"If he doesn't give us something by the next break we start the paperwork."
She nodded once, grim. "Let's ruin his evening then."
Hargreaves straightened his tie and turned for the door.
"Let's go turn the screw."

Chapter Fourteen

Friday, 21st March 2025 – 22:24

The door clicked open, and both officers re-entered, their expressions sharpened by whatever had passed between them in the corridor. Jonah looked up instinctively, his shoulders flinching at the sound, but neither Hargreaves nor McIntyre acknowledged him immediately.
They took their seats in silence. Cartwright let out a tired sigh and adjusted his chair. He looked at no one in particular. McIntyre pressed the button on the recorder.

"This interview is now resumed at 22:24 hours. All present remain the same: DS Mark Hargreaves, DC Sarah McIntyre, Mr Jonah Overaugh, and duty solicitor Mr Stephen Cartwright."
There was a brief pause as Hargreaves flipped through the pages in his file with deliberate calm. Then he spoke. Flat and direct.
"Jonah, earlier you told us you stayed at Brendan Hughes'

house all night last Friday. That you played on the Nintendo Switch in the garage and left around nine the following morning. Is that still your account?"

Jonah shifted uncomfortably in his chair. "Yeah. That's what happened."

Hargreaves nodded slowly, then reached down and retrieved a clear evidence sleeve. He slid it across the table. Inside was a printed photo: grainy and clearly from a Ring doorbell camera.

Brendan and Jonah. Walking out of Brendan's front door at 00:02.

Jonah was holding the car keys.

"Can you explain this then?" Hargreaves asked, his voice as mild as the steel edge beneath it. "This image shows you both leaving Brendan's house just after midnight. You're in the driver's seat. Brendan gets into the passenger side. Recognise it?"

Jonah stared at the photo but said nothing.

Cartwright shifted beside him, starting to look a little more focused now "You're not obliged to answer that."

McIntyre leaned forward slightly. "The same camera picks you up again at 05:14. Same car. This time, you're alone. Brendan's not with you. You drive up. Get out. Go into the house. No Brendan. No second door opening. Nothing."

Jonah swallowed hard.

"I, I, err."

"So again," Hargreaves said, "Do you want to revise your account of that night?"

Jonah's voice was barely a whisper. "No."
"You're sticking to the story that you never left Brendan's house?"
"I don't know," Jonah said, eyes fixed on the table.
McIntyre flipped open another folder marked 'DIGITAL EVIDENCE – HUGHES' and drew out a printed sheet. She laid it gently on the table between them like a playing card.
"Jonah, you said you and Brendan had your phones with you all night. That you were at his house, in the garage, playing on the Nintendo Switch. That neither of you left."
Jonah nodded slowly a flicker of hope crossing his lips, but his eyes were fixed on the page, already narrowing.

McIntyre continued, her voice calm, clipped, clinical.
"Let me walk you through what we've confirmed."
"Firstly, both mobile phones- yours and Brendan's - were found inside Brendan's house. That's true. But here's the thing, Jonah. Neither phone registered any meaningful activity after 23:58. No calls. No texts. No app use. No screen unlocks. No GPS movement. It's like both phones just... stopped. At the same moment."
Jonah hands started to tremble, a trigger that did not go unnoticed by the detectives.

Cartwright cleared his throat, though it sounded more like a cough he regretted halfway through. He shuffled the squiggle-ridden pad in front of him and finally spoke, his voice dry and brittle.
"Look, I-I think perhaps we're straying a little from... from

fact into, well, speculation. My client has already stated his position."

He glanced sideways at Jonah, then back at Hargreaves and McIntyre, his expression somewhere between apologetic and uncertain.

"And erm, if we could perhaps avoid... insinuating criminality before any charge has been laid? That would be... appreciated."

The silence that followed was brutal.

McIntyre didn't even blink. Hargreaves stared at Cartwright like he'd just walked in from the wrong interview.

"Mr Cartwright," Hargreaves said calmly, "we're not insinuating. We're investigating. If your client doesn't want the full weight of this case landing on him, now would be the time to correct the record."

Silence.

She flipped to the next sheet and tapped it.

"Secondly, the Hughes family home has fibre broadband. Standard Virgin Media router. We've pulled the event logs. Between midnight and 9am, there was no data traffic from Brendan's phone, your phone, or the Nintendo Switch or any device in Brendan's room. Nothing. No device connection pings. No user activity. No YouTube. No Mario Kart. No system checks. Not even a background update. The garage had no WiFi activity, Jonah. You two didn't play games all night. You left the phones behind. Like decoys."

Cartwright blurted again: "Err, please avoid... insinuating

criminality before any charge has been laid."
Jonah shifted in his chair, his expression now pale and frozen. His mouth worked, but nothing came out.

McIntyre didn't let up.
"Do you understand what that tells us? The phones were planted or should I say left behind. You left them there to make it look like you never left the house. Like you two were in the garage all night, having a laugh. But the Switch logs are dead. The WiFi says nothing happened. And the tower pings confirm that neither phone left that house. But clearly both of you did."
She leaned in, voice softer but sharper now.
"You made a rookie mistake. You assumed leaving the phones would be enough to build a story. But you forgot that silence speaks too."
She let that hang for a moment.
"What in this silence are you trying to hide Jonah?"
More silence.
"So, either something terrible happened to Brendan at that industrial estate, or you know who else was involved. Because you didn't just forget to mention it, Jonah. You built a lie. And lies in a case like this? That's not just obstruction. That's perverting the course of justice in a live missing persons investigation."
Jonah felt like he'd been bitten by a snake… a paralysis spreading through him. He was experiencing a new level of fear that his young life had never known before.

Cartwright coughed again, nervous and shallow. He shifted in his seat and gave a weak smile that didn't quite reach his eyes.

"Look, I think we're getting ahead of ourselves here. My client has already explained the phones were left behind, and frankly we don't know where they went, do we? We're talking about assumptions. Hypotheticals. No one's said what actually happened to Brendan."

Hargreaves turned to him slowly, expression flat, voice quiet. "You're right, Mr Cartwright. We don't know where Brendan went. But we DO know where THEY did."

He paused, turning his gaze back to Jonah, letting the silence build just long enough to make the boy squirm again.

"Jonah," he said, voice steady. "Do you know what an eSIM is?"

Jonah blinked, confused. "A what?"

McIntyre opened a new file and laid it on the table; another map, this time cleaner, digital, precise.

"It's an embedded SIM card. Built into modern vehicles. Allows things like breakdown tracking, emergency services, route data. Brendan's i10 has one."

Hargreaves continued, voice now surgical.

"Between 00:11 and 05:06 that night, Brendan's car registered to him, fitted with that eSIM was parked at Moorside Industrial Estate. Eight hundred metres behind your house. Not moving. Five hours. Just sitting there. Then it drove back. ANPR cameras caught you both leaving Brendan's road at 00:03. Same cameras caught you returning alone at 05:14."

Jonah's mouth moved but nothing came out. Cartwright

opened his own folder as if looking for something anything then just closed it again. Quietly.

McIntyre stepped in.
"So, Brendan vanishes. The car goes to a dead, silent corner of town in the middle of the night not 800 metres from your own home. You return alone. Phones left behind. No game activity. No WiFi use. Five hours unaccounted for. But you expect us to believe nothing happened?"
She leaned forward, voice lowering to a near-whisper.
"Because if we're wrong Jonah, if Brendan shows up tomorrow with some wild story about losing signal and falling asleep in a skip then fair enough. But if we're right? If something happened at that industrial estate, and you're lying about it? You need to understand something very clearly."
She paused.
"We're already three steps ahead of you."
Jonah felt as though his entire body had turned to stone: every muscle rigid. His ears rang with the blood pounding in his skull, drowning out the officer's words even as he registered their meaning. He wasn't angry. He wasn't scared in the way he'd thought fear felt.

This was different.
This was shame, panic, disbelief all folded into a dense, choking mass that sat in his throat and wouldn't move. He wanted to speak, to scream, to rewind the clock just ten minutes and find a better answer but his voice was gone. Not stolen, not silenced, just utterly absent. He was twenty

minutes away from home, and yet everything familiar felt a lifetime behind him.

Hargreaves stared across the table, fingers laced tightly in front of him, elbows square and solid against the wood. The temperature in the room seemed to shift, not physically, but emotionally. The tone had changed.

"Jonah," he said, voice low but firm, "this is your moment."

He let the silence build for a beat.

"We've presented you with evidence that contradicts nearly everything you've told us. CCTV. Phone logs. eSIM data. WiFi analysis. It's all here. Right now, you've got one last opportunity to correct the record. Come on son, do the right thing..."

Jonah's lips parted slightly. His eyes were locked on the edge of the table as if it might somehow offer him an escape route.

Cartwright didn't move, didn't speak. Just stared down at the blank page of his notepad, pen motionless in his fingers.

McIntyre leaned forward, voice precise.

"This isn't just about Brendan anymore, Jonah. This is about your integrity. Your freedom. Your future. Are you absolutely sure you don't want to change your account of what happened that night?"

Jonah's jaw worked silently. His hand twitched. But still nothing.

He couldn't speak. Couldn't lie. Couldn't tell the truth.

He just sat there, paralysed.

"Very well," Hargreaves said quietly, leaning back. "Let the record show that Mr Overaugh declines to provide further clarification."

He looked to McIntyre, who gave the smallest of nods.

"Mr Overaugh," Hargreaves continued, tone now fully official, "you are being detained on suspicion of perverting the course of justice in relation to an ongoing missing persons investigation. You do not have to say anything, but it may harm your defence if you do not mention now something you later rely on in court. Anything you do say may be given in evidence."

Cartwright finally raised his head. "You're charging him?"

"We are," McIntyre confirmed, already rising. "Interview concluded at 22:57 hours."

The red light on the recorder blinked once, then went dark. Jonah didn't move.

His world had just changed, and he hadn't even opened his mouth. As the words "You are being detained" sank in, a part of him fractured so quietly he almost didn't feel it.

Chapter Fifteen

Friday, 21st March 2025 – 23:17

Seth paced the corridor of the East Lancashire Custody Centre like a man trying to outrun the very floor beneath his feet. The strip lighting above buzzed faintly, offering no comfort, and the muted hum of the building's heating system only served to underscore how quiet everything else had become.

He had been alone for nearly two hours. Two hours since they'd disappeared into that grey-bricked maze with his son. Two hours since the door closed behind Jonah. Two hours since the weight in his chest had gone from anxiety to something dangerously close to panic.

Seth checked his watch again. The time ticked forward, oblivious. He clenched and unclenched his fists as if trying to keep the blood moving, to keep his body from shutting down entirely.

Then a door opened. Cartwright emerged, the solicitor looking more dishevelled than he had when he arrived, which Seth hadn't thought possible, but now he genuinely looked like a soaked pudding of a man. His tie was askew, collar wilted, and his briefcase hung open at one side like it had tried to escape the interview before he had.

Seth straightened immediately, moving toward him with urgency. "Well?"
Cartwright hesitated, scratching at the back of his neck. "Right. Okay. Yes. So - Jonah's been... charged."
The words struck Seth like a slap. "Charged? With what?"
Cartwright opened his mouth, then closed it again, fumbling with the clasp on his briefcase. "Err... Perverting the course of justice. In relation to the Brendan Hughes disappearance."
Seth's jaw tightened. "They think Jonah did something to Brendan?"
Cartwright shook his head. "No, no, well, yes. Not directly, but maybe. It's... they're not saying he hurt him. Not yet. They just know he was the last person to see him. But they've got data, digital stuff. Car movement logs, WiFi inactivity. Ring doorbell footage. They say he lied in interview. And err... their tone changed. Quite drastically."
Seth stepped in closer. "You're going to have to be a hell of a lot clearer than that, Mr Cartwright."
Cartwright held up both hands. "Look, I'm just relaying what I saw and heard within the bounds of what I am allowed to discuss. They say both phones, Jonah's and Brendan's, were

left at Brendan's house. No activity after midnight. Like, total digital silence. Then there's Ring footage showing them leaving the house at 00:02. Jonah was driving. Brendan in the passenger seat."

Seth blinked. "He doesn't have a licence."

"Correct," Cartwright nodded. "But I think that's the least of his problems right now. There's footage again of Jonah returning to Brendan's home alone. Same car. 05:14. No Brendan. That's what tipped the scale, I think."

Seth's voice dropped to a dangerous whisper. "Was he in Brendan's car?"

"Yes, and they tracked it using the car's eSIM," Cartwright said, voice cracking slightly. "Apparently modern cars have those now? I didn't know. They say it was parked at Moorside Industrial Estate for five hours. Then he came back. Alone. They have ANPR footage of both trips."

"Moorside industrial estate? Behind our house?"

"Yeah, that's the one, they said it was about 800 metres from his home, so it sounds like it."

Seth felt his legs weaken slightly. He reached for the nearby chair and sat, hard.

"So that's it? They're keeping him?"

"They're processing him now," Cartwright replied. "Bail wasn't even discussed. Interview ended, charge issued, remand paperwork's being done as we speak. He'll be in the holding cells here overnight for the weekend then in magistrates court Monday morning."

Seth ran a hand over his face. "And he didn't say anything? About what happened?"

"Not a word," Cartwright said. "He was… gone. Just shut down. I've seen kids go quiet, but this was different. Like he was trapped inside himself."

Seth stared at the scuffed floor tiles; his voice barely audible. "He doesn't know what happened. Because he doesn't know what happened. Now they're going to lock him up for it."

Cartwright shifted awkwardly. "Look, I'll be honest Mr Overaugh, I was caught on the back foot here. They had evidence, layers of it. They were playing chess. But I'll do what I can for him."

Seth stood again taller now, something igniting behind his tired eyes. "You're going to need to do better than that."

Cartwright nodded slowly, smoothing his tie, realising too late it was stained with what looked like coffee and regret. "Yes. Yes, of course."

"Make sure he knows he's not alone," Seth said flatly. "Whatever happens next, he needs to know that."

And without another word, Seth turned, moving toward the exit like a man heading back into a storm with no coat and no map.

Seth turned back just as Cartwright was about to disappear into the corridor.

"When can I see him?" he asked, voice low, tense with desperation.

Cartwright hesitated. "Not tonight. They'll keep him here in custody until Monday morning. First appearance will be at the Magistrates Court. Likely Preston or Blackburn depending on which rota's running."

Seth stepped closer. "So when? Tell me exactly. I need to know."

"I'll find out first thing Monday and call you the moment I have confirmation," Cartwright said, pulling out a battered notebook and scribbling furiously. "I've got your number. If there's any change before then, I'll ring, even if it's Sunday night. I promise."

Seth folded his arms, jaw clenched. "And after court?"

"If he's remanded, he'll be moved to a youth offenders institute, probably Wetherby or Thorn Cross. First visits are usually within 72 hours of transfer. I'll guide you through it."

Seth stared at him a moment longer, then gave a tight nod. "Make sure you do."

"I will," Cartwright replied, already turning away, but his tone had changed. It was quieter, steadier. "I'll keep you in the loop. You've got my word."

Cartwright watched Seth go with the quiet dread of a man who knew exactly how far out of his depth he really was.

Seth stepped out into the night air, the automatic doors hissing shut behind him like the seal on a vault. He paused beneath the sodium glow of the car park lights, staring at nothing, keys clenched tight in his fist. In his chest, hope and dread warred silently, that small, flickering belief that maybe, just maybe, this had nothing to do with what happened last Friday. That Jonah was merely caught in a horrible coincidence, a misunderstanding born of proximity and bad luck. But deep down, beneath the rationalising and denial, something darker was rising.

The evidence was stacking, the coincidences too aligned, the narrative too clean. And the terrible, inevitable truth, the one he had buried beneath ash and dirt and silence, was beginning to claw its way back to the surface.
He sat in his car and turned the engine.
The dash came to life

The time on the digital display read 00:24… Exactly one week since the incident and in that small period a fate worse than he could possibly imagine was unfolding not just to him, but for every single member of his family…
He rested his head on the steering wheel and sobbed.

Chapter Sixteen

Saturday, 22nd March 2025 – 00:24

Jonah sat slumped on a plastic bench just outside the holding cells, his limbs heavy, his thoughts adrift. The noise around him felt distant: boots on polished floors, the clipped voices of officers, the occasional rattle of keys all muffled under the thick fog of disbelief hanging in his mind.

He had stopped shivering a while ago. Now it was just a kind of hollowness as though something essential had been scooped out of him.
"Overaugh, Jonah," a voice called.
He stood automatically, muscles obeying while his brain lagged. A custody officer in his late thirties, sharp fade, bulked frame, ink visible at the collar, gestured him forward. His badge read DCO Marsden.
"Come on, lad. Let's get you processed."
Jonah nodded numbly, following.
"Stand there. Hands flat on the scanner."

Jonah placed his palms onto the glass. A dull beep followed. The screen flashed blue.

"Now the other side. Fingers."

The machine blinked and registered each print with a faint hum. Marsden jotted the numbers down into a logbook and gestured toward the wall-mounted camera.

"Look into the lens."

A bright flash burst, and Jonah flinched, blinking rapidly. His photo: blank eyes, pale skin, hair in disarray, appeared for a second on the monitor before being logged into the system.

"No tattoos or identifying marks, right?" Marsden asked flatly.

"No," Jonah mumbled.

"Alright. Belt and shoelaces off. Empty your pockets into the tray."

Jonah did as he was told, moving slowly. The tray was collected, labelled, and carried away.

He was handed a thin grey blanket and shown to a cell.

Bare concrete, one small, frosted window, steel toilet in the corner, a plastic mattress bolted to a raised platform.

It didn't smell awful. It didn't smell like anything. That was worse somehow.

The officer closed the door with a dull thud. The electronic lock clicked shut. That sound, metallic, final, made Jonah's stomach turn.

For a while, he just stood there.

Then he sat.

Then he lay down, the blanket bunched under his head, eyes fixed on the ceiling.

The stillness made space for the questions.
What had just happened?
Why the fuck had he listened to Brendan!
He could still hear Brendan's voice laughing, pitching the idea like it was nothing. "Come on man, pay dirt..."
Jonah hadn't wanted to.
But Brendan was persistent. Charming. And honestly, Jonah had wanted to prove he wasn't boring. That he wasn't just the safe, quiet one.
A little escape to freedom money, no real victim. Simple.
Now it sounded, and more importantly, felt like a trap.
They'd left the phones. They'd taken the car. Parked behind at the estate and stayed in the dark.
But he never came back. HE NEVER CAME BACK!
Jonah had waited. And waited. And then he'd panicked.
He thought that if he didn't speak about it, it wouldn't be real.
He thought silence might protect him.
But now the silence had betrayed him.
And that mother of his incessantly phoning him all week, what could he say? He had no idea where he was, that bit was true!
Jonah stared at the corner of the cell, heart thudding slow and heavy in his chest.
He should never have listened to Brendan.
And now, he had no idea where Brendan was or what the hell has happened to him.

Chapter Seventeen

Saturday, 22nd March 2025 – 00:24

Seth didn't move.
The car engine had long since fallen silent, but he sat there, motionless in the driver's seat, hands gripping the wheel as if it might somehow steer him away from the truth.
The orange glow of the nightlight outside Moorside House bathed the gravel drive in a sleepy hush. Everything looked… undisturbed. Quiet. Too quiet.
He couldn't bring himself to open the door.
He didn't want to say it aloud. Didn't want to watch the horror unfold across Natalia's face. Didn't want to see Izzy's eyes turn to panic again. Not after the week they'd had. Not after everything they'd buried. But there was no avoiding it. Not now.
Jonah had been charged.
He finally exhaled, a shuddering breath that fogged the windscreen. Then, with a slow motion that defied every instinct in his body, he reached for the door handle and

stepped out into the cold.

The house greeted him like a sleeping beast, old stone and black windows, silent and heavy. Inside, the kitchen light was on.

They were waiting.

He opened the back door quietly, as if that might soften what he was about to bring with him. The warmth of the kitchen hit him like a wall. Natalia sat at the table, still fully dressed, fingers wrapped tightly around a half-empty mug of chamomile tea. Izzy was perched on the edge of a stool, her knees tucked to her chest, hoodie sleeves pulled down over her hands. Lydia sat at her feet, head on her paws, tail thumping once when she saw Seth.

He didn't speak immediately. Just closed the door and leaned back against it, looking at the two women who loved Jonah more than anything. Who'd already lost too much sleep, too much peace.

Natalia was the first to speak. "What happened?"

Seth shook his head slowly, voice hoarse. "They've charged him."

Izzy's head snapped up. "Charged him with what?"

"Perverting the course of justice," he said. "He's being held until Monday. Magistrates Court."

Natalia's knuckles whitened around her mug. "Jesus."

"They say he lied in interview," Seth continued, slowly pulling off his coat. His movements were stiff, as if he was made of glass and could shatter if he moved too quickly. "They've got evidence. Digital evidence. Things we... we don't think about."

He sat down heavily at the table, the legs of the chair creaking beneath him.

Izzy didn't move. "What kind of evidence?"

Seth looked at her, then to Natalia. "It's bad. Their phones, Brendan's and Jonah's, were left behind at Brendan's house. No activity after midnight. Like they'd both just… gone dead. Doorbell camera caught them leaving the house just after midnight. Jonah was driving."

"He doesn't have a licence," Natalia said quietly, more to herself than anyone.

"I know. That's the least of it. There's footage of him returning at 05:14. Alone."

Natalia's lips parted slightly, a tremor starting in her hand. Izzy stared, mouth slightly agape.

"They tracked the car with its eSIM," Seth continued. "Apparently Brendan's i10 has one. It was parked at Moorside Industrial Estate, eight hundred metres behind our house. For five hours. Didn't move."

Izzy blinked slowly. "He left Brendan there?"

Seth didn't answer. He just shook his head. "He says he doesn't know what happened. But they don't believe him. Cartwright his duty solicitor… Christ, the man looked like a puddle in a tie, said Jonah just shut down. Didn't say a word."

Natalia's voice was barely above a whisper. "Do you think he knows more?"

"No," Seth said firmly. "I think he panicked. I think he made a stupid decision trying to protect someone. Or maybe he thought silence would save him. I don't know."

"But silence is what's going to bury him," Nat muttered.

The kitchen fell quiet for a moment, the weight of her words settling like dust.
Seth rubbed at his face with both hands, feeling the exhaustion of the last week collapse onto his shoulders. "I asked when I can see him. Cartwright said he'll call after court on Monday. If Jonah's remanded, he'll go to a Young Offenders' Institution. Might be Wetherby. Could be Thorn Cross. Wherever it is I'll go."
"I'm going with you," Natalia said immediately.
Izzy stood, pacing slightly, her arms folded across her chest. "So, what happens now? What if they don't believe him? What if Brendan never shows up?"
"Then we're in trouble," Seth said. "All of us. Because I think we need to be realistic, He didn't leave Brendan there, he left Brendan here…"
Izzy stopped, her eyes meeting her father's.
They all knew what he meant.
The house. The pit. The silence. The secret.
Natalia finally stood, walked to the sink and rinsed out her mug with shaking hands. "We must be perfect from now on. Every second. No mistakes. No cracks. And we must find out what happened to Brendan before the police find out what happened to him."
Seth nodded slowly.
Izzy sat again, quiet. "You're joking right? We all know what happened to Brendan… I don't see any other missing person investigations happening…"
Seth looked at her for a long time.
Izzy raised an eyebrow.

He didn't reply.

Somewhere in the distance in a cell not so far away Jonah stared at the ceiling, thinking he should never have listened to Brendan.

And now... he might never get the chance to ask where the hell Brendan had gone.

Act III

The Catalyst

Chapter Eighteen

Saturday, 1st March 2025 – Two weeks before the incident

"I'm so fucking bored, man!" Brendan proclaimed, flopping face-first onto the battered grey sofa like a toddler who'd been denied sweets. His voice was muffled by the cushion, but the drama carried regardless.

Jonah sat cross-legged on the floor, leaning against the radiator under the window, scrolling absent-mindedly through Reddit on his phone. "Yeah, and whose fault's that? You finished college a month ago, you've not applied for a single job, and you sleep 'til noon every day."

"Because jobs are for people with dead souls," Brendan replied, rolling onto his back with a groan. "I want to live, mate. Properly. Before we're like... paying council tax and pretending we care about vegan sausages and shit."

Jonah smirked but didn't look up. "You literally cried when they took your chicken nuggets off the menu at the Walton."

"That's not the point," Brendan said, propping himself up on his elbows. "I'm talking about real life stuff. Like... flying to Croatia for Ultra Festival or Ibiza or, I dunno, Barcelona, somewhere with beaches and cocktails and girls who don't say 'you remind me of my cousin'."

Jonah finally looked up. His room was a chaos of clothes, boxing gloves, a leaning tower of Coke cans, and an open packet of Reese's half melted into his desk. He raised an eyebrow. "Alright. So, we go. Flights, hotel, tickets, spending money… what's that? A grand? Two?"

"Try three," Brendan said, unlocking his phone and swiping to a saved tab. "VIP passes, private boat party, poolside suite. I priced it up last night. Three grand and change. But tell me that isn't the dream, bro."

Jonah leaned forward, taking the phone from him and scanning the screen. "Three grand for five nights of sunburn and overpriced mojitos."

"With topless Scandinavian girls on every rooftop," Brendan added with a grin.

Jonah didn't respond immediately, but Brendan caught the flicker in his eyes, the pause, the mental maths, the daydream forming.

"We deserve this," Brendan pushed. "One last bender before real life kicks in. You and me, beach clubs, international vibes, memories we want to remember."

Jonah tossed the phone back into Brendan's lap. "And how exactly are we getting three grand? My overdraft's already dead, and I'm pretty sure your bank card's only good for scraping weed resin."

Brendan dropped the phone on the floor and leaned forward. "Alright, this is where it gets spicy. I've got a plan. Don't freak

out."
"Whenever someone says, 'don't freak out', it means you absolutely should."
Brendan grinned. "We do a heist!"
"A what? We're not Bonny and Clyde"
"You'd be the girl pal…"
"Fuck off… A heist? You stupid dick!".
"No, listen…" Brendan leaned forward. "We find a mark, a soft mark, then we scope it out and then BAM, we hit it, get the readies and jet off to Croatia to lay low for a while."
Jonah rolled his eyes "You have been watching way too many cheesy gangster flicks, and I for one don't fancy going to prison for a seeing to off big Tyrone and his mates!"
"You'd love that!"
"Fuck off!"
"Dinner's ready!" Natalia shouted up the stairs.
In unison they rose to their feet and shuffled out the door and down to the kitchen.

The kitchen was warm and filled with the comforting scent of garlic, roasted vegetables and whatever spice blend Natalia had decided to experiment with that week. Brendan and Jonah sat at the island, plates loaded, while Seth stood at the hob, carving into a baked salmon fillet with his usual military precision.
"Unreal," Brendan said through a mouthful. "You guys eat like this every night?"
"Only when Nat's off work," Seth said, passing a slice of lemon to each plate. "Otherwise, it's oven chips and

complaints."

Natalia stood by the counter sorting through the unopened post, her wine glass balanced in one hand, a small pile of letters in the other. She was scanning with her usual efficiency: bills, charity appeals, and two takeaway menus she immediately lobbed into the recycling bin.

"Oh, here we go," she muttered, pausing at one white envelope. "The insurance renewal has come through."

Seth looked up from his seat, fork halfway to his mouth. "How much has it gone up this time?"

"Seven percent," she said, tearing the flap and scanning the figure. "Bastards."

Seth gave an audible huff. "That'll be all those ridiculous watch valuations, I bet."

"Probably," Natalia said, sipping her wine. "You've got half the bloody Crown Jewels in that drawer."

Brendan, eyes still fixed on his plate, gave the slightest glance toward Jonah before asking casually, "What's the insurance for again?"

"House contents. High value items," Natalia replied, without looking up. "The watches, jewellery, the paintings, all that stuff."

Brendan gave a low whistle. "Must be worth a fortune."

"Not as much as the premiums," Seth said gruffly.

Jonah gave a forced laugh and took a long drink from his glass.

The rest of the meal passed in trivial chatter. Brendan asked Seth about his Army days as usual, which launched a short story about a sandstorm and a broken satellite dish in Iraq. Natalia rolled her eyes and went back to her wine. Izzy didn't appear, she was holed up upstairs with headphones on, likely lost in TikTok or some dystopian graphic novel.

When the plates were mostly cleared and the last of the salad picked through, Brendan leaned back with a stretch.
"That was lush, Mrs O. Cheers."
"You're welcome," Natalia said with a smile. "Don't expect dessert, though. We're not running a restaurant."
Brendan nudged Jonah. "Come on, man. We've got stuff to sort."
"Homework?" Natalia asked with a smirk.
"Something like that," Jonah replied, already pushing his chair back.
They left the table and headed back upstairs. As they disappeared into the hallway, Seth looked at Natalia with a frown.
"What does he mean, 'sort stuff'?"
Natalia shrugged. "Teenage things. Probably downloading music or swapping conspiracy theories."
Seth reached for the remote and grunted. "Bloody Pornhub more like, good Lord... I hope they're not gay!"
"SETH!" Natalia scolded. Seth continued firing up Netflix.

Chapter Nineteen

Saturday, 1st March 2025 – Two weeks before the incident

Jonah had entered the bedroom first, and Brendan followed behind, slamming the door shut with his back pressed against it as if guarding a state secret.
"DUDE!" he said, his voice loud but muffled, as if the excitement couldn't quite be contained in his chest.
"What?" Jonah said, flopping onto the battered sofa, still halfway chewing the last bite of his dinner.
"What? What do you mean what? Fucking pay dirt that's what!"
Jonah frowned, blinking slowly. "What are you on about?"
Brendan gave a theatrical groan, marching across the room and standing directly in front of Jonah like a deranged motivational speaker.
"The insurance policy, you mug!"
Jonah looked even more confused. "What?"
"Stop saying what!" Brendan threw his arms into the air. "Jesus, were you not listening? Your mum said the contents

insurance renewal came through, seven percent hike because of all the high-value stuff in the house."

"Yeah, so?"

"So?" Brendan repeated incredulously. "So that means your dad's watches, the jewellery, the paintings, all of it is officially valued and insured. Which means…" He held out both hands as if revealing a magic trick, "we can take them."

Jonah stared. "You want to steal my dad's watches?"

"Not steal," Brendan said, grinning. "Liberate. Reallocate. They're insured! It's a victimless crime. The insurance company pays out, your dad gets shiny new watches, and we get a trip to Croatia with change for cocktails and designer sunglasses, no one will be any the wiser!"

Jonah scoffed. "You've lost your mind."

Brendan flopped dramatically onto the bed arms spread like he'd just landed a skydive. "Mate. Listen. Your dad doesn't even wear half of them. They're just sitting there in that big arse drawer in the bedroom untouched. You said it yourself last year, some of them are vintage collectables. We'll leave them, just take the ones we know we can sell.

"I said they're valuable watches. I didn't say let's rob them."

Brendan sat up his face animated, persuasive. "It's not robbery. It's a favour for a man like Seth. He'll get double what they're worth when the insurance kicks in. You know how it works. He submits the claim, shows the receipts, gets modern replacements. Meanwhile, we've solved our problem."

"And what if he figures it out?" Jonah asked, but his tone had softened. He wasn't dismissing it outright anymore and

Brendan noticed it.

"He won't," Brendan said, eyes gleaming. "That's the beauty of it. He'll just assume it was some random break-in. There's no forced entry, no signs of struggle, we won't even take anything else. Just the watches. In and out."

Jonah leaned forward, elbows resting on his knees. "You've really thought about this, haven't you?"

"I've done more than think about it," Brendan replied, pulling out his phone. He swiped through his gallery and held it up. A grainy, poorly lit photo of Seth's drawer full of watches stared back at Jonah.

"Jesus, when did you..."

"Last time I crashed here. Had a look while everyone was watching The Chase. You really need to lock your doors man; security round here is lax as fuck!"

Jonah rubbed his hands over his face. "You're mental."

"Yeah, But I'm right," Brendan said, undeterred. "Come on, Jonah, just think about it, no one gets hurt. Your old man gets compensated for nearly double what they are worth. We get the coin, Croatia, Girls, Sun, Freedom. What's the worst that could happen?"

Jonah sighed, leaning his head back against the wall, staring up at the cracks in the ceiling. "You realise how insane this sounds?"

"It only sounds insane because it's brilliant," Brendan said, pacing now. "Everyone dreams of doing one heist in their life. This is ours. Our Ocean's Eleven moment except it's just two of us and a fuckload less Brad Pitt."

Jonah chuckled despite himself. "You'd be the guy who trips

the alarm trying to find the snacks."

"Laugh it up," Brendan said. "But I'm serious. We can do this. All we need to do is plan it properly. No mess, no trail, no panic."

"I don't know, man..." Jonah said, hesitating again.

Brendan saw the crack and moved in. "We don't even do it together. That's the genius bit. You can't be involved directly. We'll get caught on CCTV, right? Your dad's got cameras everywhere."

Jonah nodded. "Yeah. Front, back, but nothing inside."

"Exactly. So, you stay out of it. I go in solo. You make sure the flat doors unlocked. You sit in the car, parked off-site. If I get caught, it's just some random idiot breaking in. You're in the clear."

"And if you don't get caught?"

"Then we're on a plane to the Adriatic coast sipping mojitos by sunset," Brendan grinned.

"And if you do get caught?"

"Then I take it on the chin, I'll say it was desperation and jealousy and plead for forgiveness but that won't happen man. We can make this watertight, you're the inside man, I'm the bag man."

Jonah stared at the floor, thoughts spinning faster than he could keep track of. It wasn't that he wanted to do it. It was just... so simple. So clean and very impressive. The logic was airtight. The reward massive. The risk if Brendan really pulled it off was low.

"And your cut?" Jonah asked finally, without looking up.

Brendan's eyes sparkled. "Fifty-fifty."

Jonah sighed again. "You're such a bastard."

"But a persuasive bastard."

Jonah picked up the remote and turned on the TV, but the sound barely registered. The room felt warmer now, charged with a strange electricity. Somewhere between disbelief and inevitability.

"I'll think about it," he muttered.

Brendan clapped his hands together. "That's all I needed to hear. Now let's watch Heat – get some research in."

And with that, the heist was unofficially underway.

Chapter Twenty

Sunday, 2nd March 2025 – Twelve days before the incident

The TV in Jonah's bedroom was on mute, the blue glow of his PC casting conspiratorial shadows across the wall. Brendan sat at the desk with a notebook open in front of him, tongue poking slightly from the side of his mouth like a school kid planning the ultimate science cheat sheet. Jonah paced behind him, arms folded, eyes flicking to the window every few seconds like guilt might already be watching.
"Okay," Brendan said, clicking his pen. "Let's go over this properly. No bullshit. We must get it right."
"I can't believe we're actually doing this," Jonah muttered.
"Too late to back out, sunshine," Brendan grinned, flipping the page. "Right. Step one: entry."
Jonah rubbed his temple. "The granny flat. Back left door. It's the only one without a camera. Dad never got around to wiring it after the scaffolding came down. You'll have to stay close to the wall, so the other camera doesn't pick you up"
Brendan jotted it down with a nod. "Sweet. You leave it

unlocked. No forced entry means no raised alarms."

"I'll do it the night before," Jonah added. "Just wedge it slightly so it looks shut. You won't even have to touch the lock. Just push it open."

Brendan drew a crude layout of Moorside on the page. "Nice. Now timing. We can't risk people being awake or being nosey."

Jonah sat down on the edge of the bed. "Friday night's movie night. Everyone's usually in bed by midnight. Mum doesn't like anyone being up after midnight and Lydia sleeps with Izzy, she's old now so she won't be a problem, and besides she knows you, so she'll probably just lick you, but you better take a dog chew with you just in case."

"So, I hit it just after midnight. Fifteen minutes past just to be sure" Brendan confirmed. "How long do you reckon I have?"

Jonah shrugged. "Ten, fifteen minutes. Tops. After that, you risk waking someone up, getting in and out swiftly is the key."

Brendan circled 00:15 in bold. "Alright. Now what about the stash? That watch drawer still full?"

Jonah looked uneasy. "Yeah, Top drawer. Wardrobe. Right-hand side, under the jumpers. Don't take all of them. Just the big hitters, the Panerai, the Grand Seiko, and the blue-dial Tudor. They're the newest, probably worth a few grand each."

Brendan whistled. "Are you sure your dad won't clock they're gone?"

"He'll assume they're at work. He rotates them. If he opens the drawer and sees a few still in there, he won't panic. Besides, he's more obsessed with his CCTV and garden than

what's on his wrist. When he realises that they are gone that's when he'll flip and as long as there is no evidence..."
Brendan flipped to a new page. "Right. Car."
Jonah sighed, already dreading this part. "We use your car obviously. We go out together, so it looks normal. Then you get out and I wait in the car. You do the job, come back. Done."
Brendan nodded. "So, we drive from my place. We park at Moorside Industrial Estate, I walk to the granny flat, go in, grab the goods and get out. No phones on us. Leave them in the garage so they don't give us away."
"Connected to WiFi," Jonah added. "That way it'll look like we never left."
"Smart," Brendan said. "The WiFi logs will show us connected. No movement."
"Only if we don't take them."
"I won't. Promise."
Jonah sat back. "If something goes wrong, I text you on the burner."
Brendan raised an eyebrow. "Burner?"
Jonah rolled his eyes. "You said this was a heist. We need two."
Brendan grinned. "Alright, inside man."
There was a long pause. The weight of what they were planning began to press in like damp through the wallpaper.
"What if someone sees you?" Jonah asked quietly.
Brendan thought for a moment. "Balaclava. Gloves. I'll wear all black. Move fast, stay low. I know the layout. Your mum leaves that lamp on in the hallway. It's enough to move

around without flipping switches."

"What about Lydia?"

"Chew stick laced with chicken fat. I'll drop it in the hallway. Distract her long enough."

Jonah stared at the floor, jaw clenched. "We're really doing this."

Brendan leaned forward, resting his elbows on his knees. "Mate. You leave the door. I get the gear. No one gets hurt. No one sees anything. We're gone before sunrise and your dad gets a nice fat cheque from the insurance company."

Jonah rubbed his face. "And we sell them where?"

"I've got a mate in Preston. He works in a jewellers; they take all sorts. He'll make sure they'll be no questions. Cash in hand, no paper trail."

"Just make sure he doesn't try and sell them online. My dad will be all over that!"

Brendan nodded.

Jonah didn't respond. His head was a war zone. Excitement. Fear. Guilt. Adrenaline. He glanced across the hallway through the open-door to the black basalt statue on the shelf. It stared back at him silently.

Brendan followed his gaze. "That creeps me out."

Jonah stood and walked out of his bedroom and over to the statue and picked it up, bringing it back into the room.

"What? This old thing?" he waved it in Brendan's face. "It might be worth a few bob, you know."

"Even if it was, I wouldn't touch that creepy thing, get rid of it."

Jonah walked the statue back to the sideboard and placed it down, feeling a slight exhilaration from the deception and treachery they were about to undertake.

Jonah shut the bedroom door softly. "We do this clean. One hit. Then we're out."

Brendan held out his fist.

Jonah stared at it.

Then bumped it.

The heist was officially a go.

The statue waited, watching the closed bedroom door patiently... a feint whisper trickled along the air in the hallway...

...Soon...

Chapter Twenty-One

Friday, 14th March 2025 – 20:25

The Uber pulled up outside Brendan's house.
Jonah climbed out of the back, hoodie up, hands in pockets, heart racing. The cul-de-sac was quiet. Still. The only noise was the faint buzz of a streetlamp and the soft growl of the hybrid engine as the car pulled away. He turned to face Brendan's narrow semi-detached house and took a steadying breath.

The light was still on above the door. That was a good sign.

He approached, hesitating only briefly before knocking. Three sharp taps, not too loud, not too soft.
The door opened almost instantly. Jane Hughes, Brendan's mum, stood there with a tired expression and half a chocolate biscuit in her hand. She looked him up and down.
"Evening, love," she said, stepping aside. "You boys camping in the garage again?"

"Yeah," Jonah replied quickly, voice low. "Just a few films, bit of Switch and pizza. Won't be loud."
"You never are." She gave him a kind smile. "He's in the back, doors open. Don't keep him up all night, though. He's got nothing to be tired for."
Jonah gave a tight smile and nodded, slipping past her and heading through the house. The air smelled faintly of air freshener and garlic bread. The hallway was cluttered with shoes, jackets, among unopened Amazon parcels stacked by the stairs.

He pushed through the back door and stepped into the converted garage that served as Brendan's bedroom.

It looked like the inside of a student flat had collided with a nightclub. LED strip lights glowed around the ceiling edges, casting a purple hue. Posters lined the walls, Scarface, Heat, The Town - all heist films. Brendan had even put fairy lights around a mini fridge, which hummed faintly next to a battered leather armchair.
Brendan stood in the middle of the room, arms crossed, pacing like a manager in a dressing room before a cup final.
"You're late."
"It's half eight" Jonah replied, dropping his rucksack onto the camp bed in the corner.
"Exactly," Brendan snapped. "We need precision. Not vibes."
Jonah sighed. "I can't do this if you're gonna be like this."
"Sorry," Brendan said immediately, lifting both hands. "Nerves. Just - this is it, yeah? It's real now."

There was a long pause. Jonah looked around the room, then back at Brendan.

"Tell me again this isn't completely fucking stupid."

Brendan walked over, picked up a folded piece of paper from his desk: a hand-drawn layout of Moorside. He pointed at each section, reciting like it was a mantra.

"Cameras here, here and here. You checked again, right?"

Jonah nodded. "The granny flat door is still off-grid. I wedged it like we said. Looks closed. Won't trigger anything unless someone's checking the logs."

Brendan tapped the map. "And we park here." He circled the Moorside Industrial Estate. "Off camera. No nosy neighbours. You stay in the car, doors locked, engine off."

Jonah folded his arms. "And what if someone sees you?"

"Then I run," Brendan replied, deadpan. "Or I smile and say I'm looking for my dog. Relax, man. It's in, out. No drama. You don't even leave the car."

"I hate this," Jonah muttered.

Brendan stepped in closer. "Look at me. I know it's mad. But it's clean. It's smart. You've done your bit. The unlocked door, the advice. You've covered me better than most people would. I'll do the grab, and we're out. By the time anyone realises, we'll be halfway through a mojito in Split."

Jonah closed his eyes for a moment. "Your mum thinks we're watching films."

"We are," Brendan said with a grin. "Just not the kind she'd approve of."

He tossed a hoodie at Jonah. "Come on. Get your game face on."

By 11:50, the boys were dressed in black from head to toe. Brendan's balaclava was tucked in the inside pocket of his jacket along with a dog chew and gloves. Jonah looked out through the thin window blinds, watching the minutes crawl by.

At 11:57, they opened the garage door silently and crept into the back garden. Jane's curtains were drawn. No lights upstairs.

They moved like ghosts, cutting through the side alley, ducking under the overgrown hedge at the front, and climbing into Brendan's motor.

The drive to Moorside felt like a PlayStation game to Jonah. He was anxious, scared, exhilarated and excited all at the same time.

They didn't speak. The streets were empty.

Jonah kept the radio off. Every noise, every turn, every blink of the indicators felt amplified.

When they pulled up to the edge of the industrial estate, Jonah parked the car behind a skip between two units, just as they'd planned. No cameras. No lights. The rear of Moorside House loomed in the distance, just beyond the canal bridge.

Brendan stared at the house for a long moment. "Looks different at night," he muttered.

Jonah didn't respond. He was too busy checking the time.

00:07.

"No phones?" Brendan asked.

Jonah nodded. "All left in the garage."

"Good." Brendan exhaled slowly. "Ten minutes. In, out. No heroics."

Jonah's hands tightened on the wheel. "Don't get caught. You've got the chew for Lydia?"

Brendan reached into his pocket and waved the chew stick.

Brendan opened the car door. The night air rushed in, damp and cool.

"Be right back, piece of cake" he said, pulling the balaclava onto his head in the hat like position, rolled up.

Then he was moving, walking over the canal bridge.

Jonah watched him cross as he disappeared behind the bushes that led down to the canal path. The darkness swallowed him quickly.

Jonah was alone.

He checked his watch again.

00:14.

He leaned back in the seat, heart hammering in his chest, and stared at the glowing dials on the dash. The silence in the car was deafening.

Jonah kept reciting his mantra. "Breathe, Breathe, Breathe…"

Chapter Twenty-Two

Saturday, 15th March 2025 – 00:33

Parked behind the skip at the far end of the Moorside Industrial Estate, the car felt less like a getaway vehicle now and more like a prison. Jonah sat in the driver's seat, the engine off, windows misted with the faint condensation of his breath. The darkness outside was dense, blanketing the canal path and the shadowed outline of Moorside House. He checked his watch.

00:34.
Brendan had been gone twenty minutes.
His hands gripped the steering wheel, knuckles whitening, forearms tensing every few seconds as he tried to steady himself. His breath came shallow and quick. He pressed the back of his head against the rest and exhaled slowly, trying to release the panic.

It didn't work.

Something felt wrong. Not wrong like nerves. Wrong like danger. Like weight pressing into his chest.

What if Brendan had been caught?

What if someone had woken up?

What if Lydia barked?

What if he slipped on the gravel and snapped his ankle and now lay somewhere in the dark, unconscious?

Jonah rubbed his eyes and sat forward, his forehead nearly touching the wheel. His stomach twisted. He'd barely eaten since lunchtime, but still, acid churned. The sweat at the base of his neck began to cool, causing a tremor down his spine.

01:41.

This wasn't right.

Brendan said it was ten minutes. In and out.

The plan had been simple. Foolproof. Jonah had checked the cameras, left the door open, reminded Brendan about Lydia. They had gone through it again and again!

And yet, Brendan was still gone. No police sirens, no lights, no noise.

The longer he sat there, the worse it got. Thoughts began to spiral. Had Brendan tripped the alarm? Did he break something? Was he caught on the stairs?

What if the police were already there?

What if Brendan had been dragged inside? What if he was hurt? Or hiding?

What if he had been recognised?

What if... what if…

Jonah slapped the steering wheel. Hard.

The sound echoed and startled him.

He was sweating now, palms slick. He wiped them on his joggers, repeatedly. The air in the car was thick, like he was breathing through a sponge.

He couldn't breathe, he felt like he was drowning.

02:52.

He hadn't moved. Couldn't move.

His stomach lurched. Suddenly, he fumbled with the door handle, flung it open, and stumbled out onto the gravel. He doubled over and retched, the sound wet and violent. Nothing came up except bile, which burned at his throat. He spat into the gravel, wiped his mouth with the back of his sleeve, and forced himself upright.

This couldn't be happening.

This wasn't how it was supposed to go.

Should he go and look? Help out? No. What if dad was there? What if someone saw him. This was Brendan's plan. Wasn't it? Should I go in? Should I stay? Should I go?

He climbed back into the car, slammed the door shut, and locked it. He pulled his knees to his chest and sat sideways in the seat, rocking slightly, whispering Brendan's name over and over again. Like a prayer.

"Come on, man. Come on, come on, come on..."

He couldn't leave. Not yet. He needed to wait. Brendan could still appear. Maybe he got distracted. Maybe he'd decided to take something else. Maybe he slipped out the back.

But the silence was oppressive, the silence was still there. The silence was hiding everything.

And shadowy outline of Moorside house in the distance remained.

03:23.
He was crying now. Not the loud, sobbing kind. Silent tears that streamed down his face, unchecked, pooling at the edge of his jaw. His body trembled. Every fibre of his being screamed for resolution, for something to make sense.
He thought about Brendan's laugh. The stupid way he smirked when he knew he was pushing too far. The cheeky wink. The way he had said, "Piece of cake," before disappearing into the darkness.
He was gone.
Jonah didn't know how, or why. He just knew it.
The certainty hit like a hammer to the gut.
Maybe Brendan had been caught.
Maybe someone else had caught him.
Maybe his dad...
Jonah froze.
Did his dad know?
Had he heard something? Seen something? Woken up?
Was Seth in there right now, questioning Brendan, demanding answers?
Or worse...
Jonah gripped the wheel again, tears blurring his vision.

05:02.
He needed to leave.
He had waited as long as he could.
His hands shook as he put the car into gear. He drove slowly, quietly, keeping to the side streets until he reached the main road. He didn't breathe properly all the way back to Brendan's house.
The sky was beginning to lighten. A dull grey creeping over the rooftops.

By 05:14, Jonah had pulled up outside Brendan's house.
It looked normal. The porch light was still on. The curtains still drawn. The neighbourhood was quiet.
He stepped out, legs stiff yet wobbly, body numb. He walked into the garage slowly, like a sleepwalker. It was exactly as they had left it. Cushions slightly skewed. Switch docked. Lights off.
He collapsed onto the sofa.
And broke.
The sobs came hard, tearing through him like convulsions. He gripped a cushion and screamed into it, hoping no one would hear. Tears poured freely now. He curled into himself, rocking, gasping, trying to hold on to something - anything.
Where the fuck are you, Brendan?
What happened?
Why didn't I stop you?
Why didn't I go with you?
His breath came in short bursts. Panic returned, squeezing his chest like a vice.

You can't stay here.
You can't explain this.
You can't...
Nearly three hours passed…
He had to go home, pretend everything was normal. If anything had happened, he would act shocked. He didn't know what he didn't know, but neither did anyone else. He would have to deal with whatever happened and think on his feet.

He forced himself upright, wiped his eyes, and blinked until he could see again. He grabbed his phone from the desk, ordered an Uber and then stuffed it into his pocket. He inhaled deeply and tried to steady his shaking legs.

He stepped out into the hallway, shoes squeaking faintly on the laminate.

In the kitchen, Jane was pouring herself a fresh cup of tea. She looked up and smiled warmly. "Morning, love. You're heading off?"

Jonah nodded, trying to keep his voice level. "Yeah, I left Brendan sleeping. Didn't want to wake him."

Jane chuckled, taking a sip of tea. "He's worse than a cat for sleep. I'll let him know you said bye."

Jonah managed a tight smile. "Thanks."

He stepped outside into the quiet street. His ride was already waiting, idling at the curb.

He slid into the back seat and closed the door behind him.
The engine rumbled. The car rolled forward.
The house disappeared behind him.
As they drove, the weight returned. He stared out of the

window, numb. Then a new fear crept in, slow and insidious.
His dad.
Did Seth know?
Had he seen something?
Was he waiting?
Waiting to ask questions Jonah couldn't answer.
Waiting to confront him.

Waiting with a look that would say everything without a single word.
Jonah sat back in the seat, chest hollow.
The sun was rising, and he was heading home.
To whatever waited there.

Chapter Twenty-Three

Saturday, 15th March 2025 – 08:56

The Uber rolled to a smooth stop just outside the gate. Moorside House loomed ahead, serene and unchanged in the early morning light. Birds chirped. The air was crisp. It could have been any other Saturday.

But not for Jonah.

He stepped out slowly, shoulders stiff, limbs heavy, and watched the car pull away. As the silence settled, so did the dread. He started to walk down the driveway.

"Morning, Jonah," Seth called out.

Shit, dad was in the garden, act normal.

Jonah flinched, clearly startled. "Oh-hey dad. Didn't expect to see you out here."

"Clearly," Seth said drily, a half-smile touching his lips. "What happened? Wet the bed?"

Jonah stared blankly for a moment, clearly not understanding. "Wait-what?"

Seth chuckled, "You're home early, mate. Usually, people your age only surface this early if they've had an accident and had to rush home."

Jonah rolled his eyes dramatically, shaking his head. "Hilarious, Dad. Truly."

He moved quickly past Seth, avoiding further scrutiny.

He opened the front door and immediately recoiled at the smell.

Bleach.

The smell hit him like a slap. Sharp. Acrid. Artificially clean.

He blinked as his eyes watered slightly.

The hallway was still. Too still. The hardwood floor gleamed more than usual, like it had been scrubbed to within an inch of its life. The radiator covers were wiped down. Even the skirting boards looked... newer.

Jonah crept forward.

He heard faint movement from the kitchen and followed it. Natalia stood at the sink, dressed in pyjamas, her hair scraped into a messy bun. She was wiping down an already spotless worktop with a damp cloth. There were three empty bleach bottles by the bin.

"God, what's that smell? It reeks of bleach in here!"

She looked up as he entered, and for a split second, something passed across her face. Then it vanished. Replaced by a weary smile.

"Morning, love. You're back early."

Jonah nodded, forcing a yawn. "Yeah... didn't sleep much. Thought I might as well come home."

She smiled faintly, but it didn't reach her eyes. They looked shadowed. Hollow.

"Sleep in Brendan's garage again?"

"Yeah."

"You two should stop pulling these all-nighters. It can't be good for you."

Jonah gave a tired laugh and headed for the fridge. "Just need orange juice. My throat's dry."

"Don't drink from the tap. It's... acting up. Just use the bottled stuff."

He frowned. "Right. Okay."

The bottle of juice was colder than it should have been. His hands trembled slightly as he poured it.

"Where's dad?" he asked making small talk, knowing Seth was outside in the garden.

"Garage. Sorting something."

Jonah nodded. "Cool."

But it wasn't cool. None of this was, it was damn far from cool.

He moved toward the hallway and headed upstairs. The steps creaked like always, but the house was quieter than usual.

At the landing, he paused.

The watches... Maybe he should check, if the watches where there and he would know if Brendan was successful or not, at least he'd have another scrap of information to help him make sense of this insane situation.

As he approached the entrance alcove to his parents' bedroom, he noticed Izzy's door was slightly ajar. Light spilled from the gap. I better make this look normal and check in on

her he thought, He knocked gently and pushed.
She was curled up on the bed, fully dressed, hoodie pulled over her knees, arms wrapped tight around her legs. Her eyes flicked up to him. Wide. Alert. Afraid?
"Hey," he said softly.
"Hey," she replied, voice tight.
There was a beat of silence. Her room looked untouched, but she looked like she hadn't slept.
"You alright?"
She nodded. "Just tired. Weird dreams."
"Same," he said.
He didn't believe her.
She didn't believe him.
"Cool," he said, backing out. "Just checking in."
She gave a half-smile and looked away.
Jonah retreated to the bathroom and splashed water on his face. The bleach smell was everywhere. The towels were freshly laundered. Even the soap tray had been scrubbed.

He wandered out of the bathroom and moved towards the alcove, creeping into the master bedroom, he approached the wardrobe and opened the top drawer, lifted the jumpers and saw the watch collection.
He looked through. Not one had been touched.
Not even a slight movement.
So, Brendan had not stolen the watches.
Had he even come in?
This was getting very strange.

Jonah stepped quietly out of the bedroom. His bare feet made no sound on the landing as he moved past the closed bathroom door and turned left towards the narrow staircase that led down to the old servants' wing.
The granny flat.
He hadn't meant to go this way, not at first. But something tugged at him. A tension. A need to check. To know.
Each step down was deliberate. Careful. The paint on the banister was still chipped where he and Izzy had slid down it as kids, but now the staircase felt steeper. He reached the bottom and crossed the tiled floor to the back entrance.
The door was shut.
He reached out.
Turned the handle.
Locked.
His pulse skipped. He jiggled it again to be sure, then stepped back, staring.
It was locked.
That door was never locked.
No one ever used it. It wasn't even connected to the alarm system, not since the rewiring years ago. Seth had meant to fix that, but like half the projects around the house, it had become another good intention gathering dust.
He'd left that door open. He knew he had. Slightly ajar. Wedged just enough to stay shut but not latch.
But someone had found it.

Someone had noticed.

And someone had locked it.

Jonah stood frozen, the implications crawling over his skin like cold water. No one ever checked that side of the house. Not his mum. Not Izzy. Not even Lydia ventured down here anymore.

Who had come down?

Who had seen?

And why had they locked it, without saying a word?

A knot tightened in his chest. The silence in the house grew heavier.

Something had happened.

Did Brendan lock it? Was it before or after he had been in the house? If it was after, then why were the watches still there? Which door did he leave through?

No one had said anything, no one said anything had occurred last night.

Where the hell was Brendan?

Downstairs again, he passed the front door and saw Seth hunched over the garden fire pit. Smoke drifted lazily into the air. Seth was wearing gloves, but when he turned slightly his right-hand glove was under his armpit and he was using the palm of his right hand to wipe his face, Jonah caught sight of red raw grazes across his knuckles. Deep, swollen cuts. Angry. Fresh.

Jonah swallowed.

Seth looked up. Their eyes met.

"You alright?"

"Yeah," Jonah replied too quickly. "You?"

Seth nodded. "Just burning some old paperwork and stuff. Spring clean. Going to be doing it all week to keep on top of it."

Jonah stepped back inside and closed the door.

He sat in the snug and stared at the blank TV.

Something had happened.

Something was wrong.

The house was too quiet.

Too clean.

Too... tense.

He went over the plan repeatedly in his head. Brendan had gone in. Jonah had waited. Brendan hadn't come out.

And now the house smelled like bleach.

His dad had cuts on his hand.

Izzy was acting jumpy.

His mum looked like she'd been on a marathon cleaning session.

It was too quiet.

Who had locked that door? Was it before or after? Why were the watches still there?

He lay back, forcing himself to appear relaxed. Pretending to nap. Pretending not to notice.

But every fibre of his body was coiled.

Ready.

Waiting.

He moved upstairs to his bedroom where he could think, think about all this insane stuff.

He lay down on his bed and the adrenaline started to wane.

He slipped into a momentary sleep.
His phone buzzed.
Jonah sat up slowly, blinking.
The screen lit up with a name:
Jane Hughes
His chest tightened. He answered.
"Hi, Jane."
Her voice was gentle, worried.
"Hi sweetheart. Is Brendan with you? When I went in to wake him up, he wasn't there, his phone is still here and he's not in his car. Is he with you?"
Jonah's blood turned to ice.
He opened his mouth. "No Mrs Hughes, I'm here alone, he must have gone to the shop or something."
"Without his phone?"
"Yeah – I guess..."
"Ok, if he contacts you tell him to ring me, we're supposed to be going out for a Chinese later on."
"No worries, Mrs Hughes, will do."
"Thanks, bye love!"
"Bye" Jonah hung up.
He sat starting across his bedroom with a vacant expression on his face. This was a complication he never saw coming. He had the sinking feeling that all of this was only going to get worse, much worse.
He heard the front door opening, it was Seth. He needed to get out of here and quick, the less time he spent here the better. He leant out of the window.
"Hey, Dad! Where are you heading?"

"Just heading to Costco. Need to replace the DVRs."
"Mind if I tag along?" Jonah called down, already halfway through the window.
Seth hesitated. "Sure. I'll wait in the car."
Within moments, Jonah emerged from the house, pulling on his hoodie and climbing into the passenger seat beside his father, trying his best to be cheerful and oblivious.
"Ready when you are," Jonah announced, distractedly checking his phone, another text from Jane.

They drove quietly towards Whinney Hill tip first, an awkward silence filling the vehicle. Jonah's eyes narrowed slightly as Seth parked by the skips, pulling out the mangled DVRs and tossing them unceremoniously into the electronics disposal bin. He noted that they looked destroyed.

His dad NEVER threw away old electronics. They have a specific set of boxes in the attic which house generations worth of old tech crap that he horded, just in case he ever needed an old connector or a wire. Why were these DVRs any different? Why was he breaking the habit of a lifetime?
"Dad, those DVRs looked wrecked," Jonah observed, lifting an eyebrow.
Seth laughed lightly, attempting to sound casual.
"You can never be too careful destroying hard drives, Jonah. Better safe than sorry. Anyway, I'm switching us over to those cloud-based Ping cameras. Much better image quality, more secure."

Jonah nodded slowly, not fully paying attention, eyes fixed on his phone.
Yet another text from Jane. He was ignoring them now.
"Sure, whatever you think best." Jonah proclaimed
If his dad had destroyed the cameras this morning, then... then... any footage from last night would not exist anymore! Sweet!
Jonah took that as his first and only sign that things might actually be looking up for him.
He was wrong, very wrong.

Chapter Twenty-Four

Saturday, 15th March 2025 – 20:47

The snug was warm. Almost too warm.
Jonah sat on the edge of the sofa, pretending to be absorbed in the TV. Some dull nature documentary flickered across the screen, narration soft, ambient forgettable. Lydia lay curled at Izzy's feet as per usual. Natalia was curled in a throw, occasionally sipping from her herbal tea, eyes half-shut. Seth, arms crossed, head tilted back, looked like he was nodding off.

Jonah had barely looked at the screen. He was too busy pretending not to look at his phone.
12 text messages.
Two missed calls.
All from Jane Hughes.

The texts started calm: "Hey, is Brendan with you? Did he turn up?" Then: "Can you ask him to call me please?" And later: "Jonah I need to know where he is. I'm getting really worried. I've called the Police"

The calls came after that. The last voicemail was short. Just her voice, cracking: "Please, Jonah. I need to know where my son is."

He didn't reply. Couldn't. Not yet.

His heart pounded every time the phone buzzed. And every time, he shoved it deeper into his hoodie pocket and faked a casual glance at the screen.

"I think we should all call it a night," Natalia said, breaking the spell. Her voice was thick with fatigue.

Seth nodded. "Good idea. I'm knackered."

Izzy gave a vague noise of agreement.

Jonah stood slowly. "Yeah, same. Think the late nights are catching up with me."

They each peeled off in turn. Natalia kissed Izzy on the head and gave Jonah a tired look before disappearing upstairs. Seth followed. Izzy lingered a few seconds longer, then padded up behind them.

No one said what they were really thinking.

No one mentioned Brendan.

No one asked why the house still smelled faintly of bleach.

Each of them climbed the stairs, alone with their thoughts, their secrets tucked away like loaded guns under the pillow.

Jonah collapsed onto his bed fully clothed, staring at the ceiling, the heavy silence in the house pressing down on him, closing his eyes into a sleep oblivion.

Outside his room, the black basalt statue watched everything.

The dream came fast.

He was standing at the edge of the long, sloping field in front of Moorside House. The sky was slate grey, the wind low and endless, humming a constant dull note through the tall grass. The trees at the far edge bent in eerie unison, like silent mourners bowing to some unseen force.

A little girl in a white nightgown ran through the tall grass, barefoot and frantic. Her feet barely touched the ground as she darted through the field, small arms pumping at her sides. Her hair streamed behind her like a ribbon, wild and golden, catching what little light bled through the sky. She couldn't have been more than six or seven.

Jonah tried to move, to call out, but his body wouldn't obey. His feet felt anchored in place, his voice stolen. He stood paralysed, watching as the scene unfolded before him like a memory he didn't know he had.

A battered 1940s van sat idling just outside the house - military green, with dull red lettering faded beyond recognition. The rear doors were ajar, yawning like an open mouth. Exhaust sputtered in faint white puffs from a crooked pipe. The house looked the same in shape, but aged - its stone less weathered and more grandiose, windows black and lifeless like the sockets of a skull. It looked abandoned, yet watching.

The girl stumbled, her foot catching on something buried in

the grass, and went down to one knee. But she scrambled up again almost immediately, glancing back over her shoulder. Her face turned briefly toward Jonah.
He saw it clearly.
Pale skin. Dirt smudged across her cheek. Eyes wide with terror and something else. Recognition.

Then came the scream.
"LOTTIE!"
A woman's voice, distant but piercing. Desperation carved into every syllable.
"Lottie! Come back!"
The girl didn't stop. If anything, she ran harder, as though the voice behind her was not a comfort but a threat.
And then, from the edge of the treeline, something moved.
A figure exploded out of the shadows. Male. Tall. Lythe. Dressed in dark wool, silhouette jagged and wrong. The face was obscured - just a smudge of shadow beneath a brimmed hat. No eyes, no mouth. Just presence.
He didn't run like a person.
He flowed.
He crossed the field in moments, his limbs long and purposeful. He closed the distance with terrifying speed, and just as the girl looked back one final time, he lunged.

He tackled her to the ground, arms locking around her waist in a bone-snapping grip. Her scream was cut off, muffled by the sudden crush of earth and force.
Jonah felt the scream tear from his own throat.

But no sound came out.
And then the man turned his head - slowly, deliberately - towards Jonah.
Even from across the field, Jonah felt the weight of that eyeless stare.
And snapped awake.

Sunday, 16th March 2025 – 07:24

It was starting to become light outside.
His heart thundered. Sweat soaked the back of his neck.
He stumbled out of bed and down the stairs, legs rubbery, throat dry.
As he reached the kitchen, he stopped suddenly.
They were all there.
Seth. Natalia. Izzy.
Sitting around the kitchen table, each with a mug of coffee in hand, faces pale, expressions vacant. No one spoke. No one moved. They just sat, staring into nothing.
"What are you all doing down here?" Jonah asked, his voice hoarse.
Natalia blinked slowly, like she was waking from a trance. "Couldn't sleep."
Seth grunted in agreement.

Izzy looked at Jonah for a long moment, then dropped her gaze to her cup.
Jonah nodded slowly and backed out of the room.

His phone buzzed in his pocket.
He pulled it out.

Missed Call: Unknown Caller
1 Voicemail

His blood chilled.
He tapped play.
"Hello, Jonah. This is Detective Constable Sarah McIntyre from East Lancashire CID. I'm trying to get in touch with you regarding Brendan Hughes. His mother has reported him missing, and you were listed as the last person to have seen him. Could you give me a call back at your earliest convenience, please? The number is 016..."
The message ended. Jonah stood frozen, phone still in hand.
It was happening.
Really happening.
He backed up the stairs, phone pressed tight to his chest.
In his room, he sat on the edge of the bed and stared at the number. His thumb hovered over the dial button.
He had to do this and get it over with, and besides he wasn't lying. He genuinely had no idea where Brendan was and lying was a lot different to not telling them everything.
Yeah, I'll go with that, he thought desperately trying to convince himself.
He swallowed.
And called.
The phone rang twice.
"DC McIntyre speaking."

"Hi. Uh, this is Jonah... Jonah Overaugh. I... got your message."

"Thanks for calling back, Jonah. I just need to ask a few quick questions. Nothing formal at this stage, okay? Brendan's mother is really worried about him and after looking at his standard behaviour patterns we are starting to get concerned as well."

"Okay."

"When did you last see Brendan Hughes?"

Jonah took a breath. He stuck to the story.

"Friday night. I stayed over at his place. We were in the garage playing the Switch all night. He went to bed. I left the next morning around nine."

"Was he still asleep when you left?"

"Yeah. I said goodbye to his mum on the way out. Brendan was in bed."

McIntyre paused. "And you haven't seen or heard from him since?"

"No. Nothing. I figured he was still asleep when Jane texted."

"Alright. Thanks, Jonah. That helps us establish the timeline. If anything comes to you, anything at all, please call me directly."

"I will."

"Have a good day."

"You too."

Jonah stared at the phone screen long after the call had ended, McIntyre's voice still echoing in his ears.

He had lied. Every word. Smooth, steady.

He'd told her they were in the garage playing Switch.

Told her Brendan went to bed.
Told her he left in the morning.
Told her Brendan was asleep.
But Brendan hadn't gone to bed. He hadn't even made it back.
And Jonah didn't just lie to protect Brendan.
He lied to protect himself.
The guilt sat like a brick on his chest. Not just the guilt of lying, but the fear of what it meant to be good at it.
He hadn't stammered.
Hadn't hesitated.
He'd sounded exactly like a boy with nothing to hide.
That scared him more than anything.
He wanted to tell the truth. He really did. But how could he? How could he explain the plan without incriminating himself?
How could he say Brendan never made it back, without raising questions about the door?
About the car?
About the time?
How was he supposed to explain to his family that they had cooked up a plan to rob them? He doubted his dad would agree that it was a victimless crime. How could he have been so stupid!
His silence was a wall now, not a shield. And it was starting to crack.
He didn't know where Brendan was.
Didn't know what his mum, dad or sister knew - if anything.
Didn't even know if the house itself had swallowed Brendan

whole. Had he fallen in the canal?
Jonah gripped the phone tighter, knuckles white.
He was in it now.
The lie had weight.
It had shape.
And it was only going to grow.

Act IV

The Silence we Hide

Chapter Twenty-Five

Monday, 24th March 2025 – 05:46

The dream came fast

Seth was moving, though he hadn't decided to. His legs walked with grim purpose; his arms swung with control he hadn't given. The world around him was bleached grey, the trees brittle and black, bowing inward like old bones. He tried to stop. Tried to speak.
He couldn't.
He wasn't in control.
He was watching.
Inside.
Trapped in his own skull - but not alone.
The field rolled out before him, wide and open, the familiar slope leading down to the silhouette of Moorside House. But it wasn't Moorside as he knew it. It was sharper. Older. Predatory. Its windows were darker than night, its chimneys bent like horns.

And at the edge of the field, a girl ran.
White nightgown. Bare feet. Hair like sunlit hay.
She ran like her life depended on it. Because it did.
Don't… he thought or tried to. Stop. Please, stop.
But the body kept moving. Gliding with a truly evil intent.
Long strides, too smooth. Not his gait, not his rhythm.
The long black coat swayed at his sides. The hat clung low over his brow. He could feel the weight of the clothes, the brush of them against his skin. Yet they weren't his.
They were his body's.
But not his choice. This wasn't him.
He screamed inside, but nothing changed. His fists clenched and unclenched, hands far stronger than he remembered.
I'm not doing this. I'm not doing this!
Still, the chase continued.
"LOTTIE!" a voice cried out behind them, distant and heartbroken.
It echoed like wind through bone. It meant something. Seth didn't know what. The girl didn't stop.
And neither did he.
His body closed the gap with terrifying ease. Each stride effortless. The grass seemed to part for him.
The girl's breath came ragged now. Her tiny frame pumped with panic.
Seth watched in horror as his hands - those hands - reached out in front of him. Large. Rough. Inevitable.
Please don't. Please, not her. Not a child-
He lunged.
The moment stretched.

She turned her head. Her eyes met his.
And Seth saw something worse than fear.
She recognised him.
Then he struck.
Arms coiled around her waist, driving her into the earth with brutal, merciless force. Her breath exploded from her lungs. Her limbs thrashed. But his grip held. Steady. Mechanical.
Seth screamed in his mind, thrashing, pounding against the walls of his own consciousness. But he was just a passenger. Trapped behind the eyes. Forced to watch.
The girl whimpered once more. Then went limp.
The sound stopped.
The field grew quiet.
And something inside the ground shifted.
Welcoming.
Satisfied.
Seth's head turned. Not by his own will.
Toward the house.
And there it was. The statue.
The black basalt figure stood tall at the edge of the field. Taller than any man, its head bowed, arms wrapped in shadow. No face. No eyes. And yet Seth felt it looking directly into him. Into whatever part of him was still his.
The wind twisted unnaturally. The sky split above.
And the voice came, not spoken but felt. Felt through bone and nerve and soul.
"You're mine now."
Seth woke with a start, bolt upright in bed, lungs dragging in air like he'd been drowning.

Sweat coated his chest. His hands trembled.
He looked down at them.
Still his.
But for how much longer?
The sheets were damp with sweat, his fists clenched tight against his thighs. A single name pulsed in his chest, louder than breath.
Lottie.
Beside him, Natalia lurched upright with a sharp gasp.
They sat in silence for a beat, the silence that crackles before a storm.
Seth turned to her. She was pale in the dim light, eyes wide and unfocused.
"You, okay?" he asked, voice gravelled.
Natalia blinked at him, then nodded shakily. "Yeah. Just… a dream."
Seth wiped his face with his forearm. "Me too."
They stared at one another, an unspoken charge hanging between them.
"What was yours?" she asked, hesitant.
Seth hesitated too, like saying it out loud might make it real. "I was outside. The field. In front of the house. Foggy, kind of grey. And there was a little girl. Running. White nightgown. Blonde hair."
Natalia stiffened. "Lottie."
The word hit like a dropped stone in a still pond.
Seth looked at her sharply. "You saw her too?"
"I've been dreaming about her for nights," she whispered.

"I didn't say anything because I thought - I don't know - I thought it was stress, or guilt, or..."
They stared at each other again, the air between them suddenly heavier, colder.
"I wasn't just watching" Seth said, quietly. "I was the man chasing her. The figure in the coat. I couldn't stop it, Nat. I wasn't in control. I was... there, but not."
Natalia's eyes filled with something colder than fear: recognition.
Seth looked down at his hands. They were trembling.
"I knew what I was doing, but I couldn't stop it. It wasn't just a dream. It was like I was inside something else. Something using me."
Natalia wrapped her arms around herself. "This isn't just stress. This isn't our minds processing trauma."
"No," Seth said, voice tight. "This is something else. Something wrong."
They sat in silence for a long time, the weight of their shared experience pressing in from every side. Moorside House seemed to hum faintly around them, as if it was listening.
Finally, Seth spoke again. "That statue was in the dream this time. It's the statue. It must be."
Natalia didn't argue.
She stood and moved towards the door and went downstairs.
Natalia stood by the kitchen sink, hands gripping the edge with white-knuckled tension. The morning light bled across the counter, catching flecks of dust in the air, but it didn't warm her. It felt cold. A type of cold that lived inside stone.
Seth was at the back door, halfway into his boots, mug of

coffee steaming at his side.

"Can you do me a favour?" Natalia said without turning.

He looked up. "Sure. What's up?"

"The statue," she said flatly. "I want it gone."

Seth frowned. "Gone where? It's on the house ledger; it's part of the Grade II listing..."

"The shed," she said quickly. Too quickly. "Just out of this house."

There was a pause. Not long. But long enough for something unsaid to fill the air.

Seth stepped further into the kitchen. "Your right. I'll move it now"

Natalia turned then, her eyes raw, voice steadier than she felt. "I don't know. But every time I walk past it, I feel like I'm being watched. And not just watched but judged. Measured. Like it knows what we did."

Seth was quiet.

Natalia continued. "Since that night, I haven't been able to sleep properly. The dreams, the feelings, the rage... I feel like it's still here, Seth. Not in the walls. Not in the air. In that thing."

He looked past her, towards the sideboard where the black basalt figure stood. Unmoving. Unchanged.

"You think it's the cause?" he asked.

"I think it's a focus," she said. "Or a trigger. Or maybe it just... remembers."

Another pause.

Then Seth nodded.

"Alright," he said. "I'll take it out to the shed after we get back from court."

"No," Natalia said quickly. "Now. Please. Before we go. I don't want to come home to that thing looking at me."

Seth didn't argue. He crossed the kitchen, picked up the statue. It was heavier than it looked. Always had been.

As he turned toward the door, Natalia stopped him with a whisper.

"Be careful," she said. "Don't... I don't know... Just don't treat it like it's just a rock."

Seth met her eyes. There was no mockery in his look.

"I haven't thought of it as just a rock in days," he said.

Then he stepped out into the cold, heading for the shed.

Behind him, the house seemed to exhale.

Seth stepped onto the gravel, the black basalt statue tucked beneath one arm, wrapped in an old tea towel like something fragile. It was heavier today. Not just in weight, but in presence. Like it knew it was being banished. Like it disapproved.

The air bit at his skin, but he didn't shiver. He moved quickly, the sound of his boots on the frosted gravel the only noise in the stillness.

The shed loomed ahead, unpainted and weathered by rain. He fumbled with the latch. His fingers felt clumsy. Numb. He wasn't sure if it was the cold or the dread.

Inside, it was dark and musty, smelling of damp wood and engine oil. Gardening tools hung from old nails. Plastic storage boxes stacked three high in the corner. The lawnmower sat like a forgotten relic in the shadows.

The saw, that saw, was hanging from the wall, pristine. Seth shuddered.

He set the statue on the highest shelf, behind a stack of paint cans, its hooded head just visible over the rim. He didn't unwrap it. Couldn't. The tea towel stayed, shrouding it like a burial cloth.

He stepped back.

The statue didn't move.

But something inside Seth whispered:

"You're mine now."

He locked the shed and stood for a moment, staring at the door, the key warm in his hand despite the cold. Then he turned and walked towards the house.

Natalia was in the kitchen, moving on autopilot. The kettle was already boiled, mugs lined up like soldiers. She was buttering toast, methodically, mechanically, her mind clearly elsewhere. The kitchen was too clean again. Bleach still clung faintly to the air, mixed now with toast and strong coffee.

She looked up when Seth stepped in. His expression told her what she needed to know.

"Is it done?" she asked.

He nodded. "It's out in the shed. Covered and tucked behind the paint cans."

"Good," she said quietly, sliding the toast onto a plate. "I don't want it near Izzy."

Seth reached for a mug. "She'll notice it's gone."

"Then we say it cracked," she replied. "Or it felt wrong after the break-in. Something. Anything. Just not the truth."

He didn't argue.

The clock ticked above the cooker. 07:12.

"Are you going to wear a suit?" Natalia asked, not looking up.

Seth shook his head. "No time to iron it. Besides, I think seeing me in a suit will just make him more nervous. I'll go smart casual."

She gave a humourless chuckle. "Very parental. Shame the rest of this is anything but."

Seth poured two coffees and handed one to her. "How's Izzy?"

"Dressed. Quiet. She's got her headphones in upstairs. I think she's trying to pretend it's just a Monday."

He nodded. "Maybe we should too."

Natalia looked at him then. Properly. Her eyes were red around the edges, makeup-free and stark.

"I'm terrified, Seth."

He stepped close, placing a hand on her lower back.

"So am I."

They stood like that for a few moments, the house creaking softly above them, the smell of toast growing slightly too burnt, neither moving to fix it.

"I keep thinking we should have told him."

Seth's hand tensed.

"Told him what? That we killed a man that attacked Izzy after he'd broken in. That we buried a body and burned evidence, while he sat waiting in a car with his mate across the canal doing god only knows what?"

Natalia didn't flinch. "No. Told him he could tell us anything. That no matter how bad it was, we'd face it together."

Seth said nothing.

She pulled away and flicked off the toaster. The smell of

singed crust filled the kitchen.

"I feel like we've already lost him," she said.

"You haven't" Izzy said quietly from the doorway.

They both turned. Izzy stood there, dressed in black jeans, her usual hoodie swapped for a dark coat. Her hair was in a braid. She looked older somehow.

"He's still him," she said. "He's just scared."

Seth reached for his keys. "We're all scared."

Natalia put a slice of unburnt toast on a plate and slid it across the counter. "Eat something, Izzy."

She took it without a word.

By 07:45, they were ready. The house was locked, jackets on, phones charged.

As they stepped out onto the drive, Natalia looked back at the kitchen window once more. She half expected to see the statue still sitting there. Watching.

But it wasn't.

And somehow, that was worse.

Chapter Twenty-Six

Monday, 24th March 2025 – 08:41

East Lancashire Magistrates' Court – Blackburn

The car pulled into the car park. Seth killed the engine and gripped the steering wheel, just for a second longer than he needed to. It was automatic. Like bracing before impact.
Natalia sat beside him, hands clamped around the leather strap of her handbag. She hadn't spoken since they left the petrol station. Not since Izzy had climbed into the back seat with a cup of tea and a silence that felt a lot older than she was.
Now, as they sat facing the back of East Lancashire Magistrates' Court, the weight of what was about to happen pressed down on them.
The building was squat and red-bricked, modern in design but not in spirit. No pillars. No ornate carvings. Just flat walls, security cameras, and a sign too clean to feel welcoming. It looked more like a crematorium than a court

of law.

"Are we ready?" Seth asked, his voice too even.

"No," Natalia said. "But let's go."

Just like the police station the lobby smelt faintly of bleach and vending machine coffee. A wall of reinforced glass divided them from security. The guards were polite but distant, dressed in dark grey polos and stab vests. Everyone's bag was scanned. Belts off. Phones in trays.

"First floor for courtrooms one to three," the security officer directed, handing Natalia her handbag.

"Thank you," she replied automatically, though she didn't feel thankful at all.

They followed the signs upstairs; their footsteps muted against the grey industrial carpet. The corridor on the first floor was long and harshly lit, lined with hard plastic benches and closed doors with small plaques: Court 1. Court 3. Interview Room 3. Probation Suite.

Each door felt like a threshold to a version of their son they hadn't met yet.

Natalia had expected the court to be bigger. Louder. Something with wood panelling and sharp-suited barristers bustling around in a chaos of folders and wigs. But this was small. Civil. Bureaucratic.

Everything was quiet here. Unnervingly so.

A court usher in a navy jacket approached them with a clipboard. Her tone was soft but clinical.

"Overaugh?"

"Yes," Seth said.

"You're here for Jonah Overaugh's appearance?"

"We are," Natalia said.

"He'll be heard in Court Two. Should be shortly. The CPS is reviewing paperwork now. You'll be seated at the back. You won't be able to speak to him unless permission is granted by the presiding bench. Do you have a solicitor present?"

Seth nodded. "Cartwright. Duty brief."

The usher gave a subtle grimace. "He's already inside. You'll be called shortly. There's a drinks machine by the waiting area if you need anything."

"Thanks," Natalia murmured.

They found a bench. Izzy sat between them, clutching a water bottle like it was a lifeline. She hadn't said anything since they entered the building.

Seth leaned forward, elbows on his knees. He didn't speak. Didn't fidget. Just stared at the grey carpet between his shoes like it held answers.

Natalia reached into her bag and pulled out Jonah's old inhaler. It was empty, long expired, but she kept it anyway. She turned it over in her palm, the faded sticker worn to blankness. It was a stupid thing, but it grounded her. It was her baby boy's.

After what felt like an eternity - though the wall clock said it had only been eleven minutes - the usher reappeared.

"You can come through now. Court Two."

Natalia stood first. Her legs felt stiff, like she'd been sitting for hours. Seth followed. Izzy trailed behind them, her expression unreadable.

Inside, the courtroom was even smaller than expected. A simple chamber with a raised bench at the front, where three magistrates sat - two women, one man. No wigs. No ceremony. Just solemnity.

To the left was the CPS prosecutor, standing behind a desk with a laptop and an overstuffed folder, that also seemed rather organised.

To the right: Cartwright. Dishevelled, already sweating. He gave them a brief nod as they entered, his eyes darting nervously toward the bench.

And at the centre - below the magistrates, behind a glass-panelled dock - stood Jonah.

Izzy gasped softly.

Natalia clutched Seth's arm.

He looked small in the dock. Smaller than he had in months. The grey jumper he wore was too loose around the shoulders, the standard-issue track bottoms bunching at the waist. His hair was flat. Eyes red. Face pale.

He didn't look at them.

The usher gestured for them to take seats at the back row.

"Jonah Overaugh," the court clerk began, her voice clear and professional, "You are before the court today in relation to a charge of perverting the course of justice, arising from the investigation into the disappearance of Brendan Hughes."

Natalia felt the words strike like iron.

Seth's jaw flexed, his fists clenched on his thighs.

Jonah didn't react. Not outwardly.

But Natalia saw the smallest twitch, just beneath his right eye.

And she knew he was hanging on by a thread.

The lead magistrate looked up from the case file, adjusting her glasses.

"We'll now hear from the Crown regarding the question of bail."

The CPS prosecutor stood. A woman in her late thirties, razor-sharp suit, hair tied back, voice crisp.

"Thank you, Ma'am. The Crown opposes bail in this matter on several key grounds, all of which indicate a substantial risk in releasing the defendant at this time."

She took a slow breath, then began.

"Firstly, the charge before the court is perverting the course of justice - an extremely serious offence which strikes at the very heart of our legal system. This is not a technicality. This is a deliberate, orchestrated falsehood provided during a missing persons investigation that remains active and unresolved."

Natalia swallowed. She could feel Seth tense beside her.

"Mr Overaugh was by his own admission, the last known person to see Brendan Hughes, who has now been missing for over nine days. His initial statement to the police claimed he and Mr Hughes spent the night playing video games, that Mr Hughes was asleep when he left the house, and that everything was normal. However, this account has been directly contradicted by independent evidence."

She lifted a page from her folder.

"Specifically: CCTV footage from a neighbouring property confirms that the defendant and Mr Hughes left the premises just after midnight, approximately five hours earlier than claimed.

"Mobile phone logs show deliberate inactivity consistent with an attempt to fabricate an alibi. And most notably, Mr

Hughes vehicle was tracked via its embedded eSIM system, placing it at a derelict industrial estate behind Mr Overaugh's residence for several hours that same night.

"When the vehicle returned at 05:14 it was Mr Overaugh alone in the driver's seat."

A murmur went through the room.

Jonah's head lowered.

Seth's fists clenched harder.

The prosecutor continued.

"At no point in his interview did the defendant mention this journey, nor offer any explanation for the contradiction. When confronted with the evidence, he chose to remain silent and maintain his false narrative."

She looked directly at the bench.

"This is not the behaviour of a confused teenager. This is the behaviour of someone actively attempting to obstruct a missing persons inquiry. The Crown believes the defendant may have knowledge of Mr Hughes' whereabouts, or fate, which he is unwilling to share."

She let that linger.

"Further, we have concerns about potential witness interference. The defendant has already demonstrated a willingness to lie, and we have reason to believe he may attempt to dissuade or influence others who were in contact with Mr Hughes in the days leading up to his disappearance. The investigation is ongoing. We cannot afford the risk of additional obstruction."

She closed her folder. "In summary, Ma'am, the Crown requests that the defendant be remanded into custody pending the outcome of the investigation and any potential further charges."

The magistrate nodded, then turned. "Mr Cartwright?"

There was a beat of silence.

Cartwright jerked upright like he'd temporarily forgotten where he was. His papers were scattered. He fumbled to gather them.

"Uh... yes, thank you, Ma'am... if I may..."

He stood, glasses slipping slightly down his nose.

"The defence... uh... does not agree... respectfully... with the, um, Crown's position."

He paused, flipping through notes, one page upside down.

"My client... Mr Overaugh... is... err... eighteen years old. No previous convictions. He has been fully cooperative with police..."

He glanced at Jonah, who stared blankly ahead.

"He's... he's not a flight risk. He lives at home with two very respectable parents, present in court today, and has deep ties to the local community. He's... uh...well-known. Well-liked."

The magistrates said nothing. Cartwright panicked and went on.

"Furthermore, there's no, uh, suggestion that he committed a violent offence. He's not being accused of harm, only of... of not telling the full truth."

The prosecutor raised an eyebrow.

Cartwright looked back at his notes. "He... uh... regrets that. Deeply. And would like to apologise for any confusion caused."

Seth visibly winced.

Natalia buried her face in her hands.

"In addition," Cartwright went on, "we believe the Crown's case relies heavily on circumstantial… that is, not definitive… um… we're not convinced that… the car, for example, doesn't…"

He trailed off.

"Uh… we respectfully ask that bail be granted with conditions, perhaps including… a… curfew… or electronic monitoring if necessary."

He nodded, far too enthusiastically. "Yes. Monitoring."

The magistrates leaned into one another for a brief, whispered exchange.

Jonah closed his eyes.

Izzy had stopped breathing.

Finally, the lead magistrate straightened and looked toward the dock.

"Mr Overaugh, we have considered the representations of both the Crown and the defence. It is clear you are facing a serious allegation connected to the disappearance of a young man who remains unaccounted for. The evidence against you, though not determinative, is compelling at this stage and raises significant concerns."

She paused.

"Given your dishonesty in interview, the unexplained vehicle movement, and your position as the last confirmed person to see Mr Hughes, we believe there is a real risk of witness interference and further obstruction."

Jonah's eyes opened. Slowly.

"We therefore decline to grant bail. You will be remanded

into custody while further inquiries are made. Your case will be escalated to Crown Court for full trial consideration. You will be held at a secure youth detention facility until your next appearance."

Seth stood. "Ma'am..."

"Mr Overaugh," the magistrate said firmly. "This is not a public address. Please sit."

Seth sat. Jaw locked.

The usher stepped forward, hand on the door release for the glass dock.

Jonah didn't move.

He looked up. Just once.

His eyes found his mother's.

And then he was gone.

Chapter Twenty-Seven

Monday, 24th March 2025 – 10:16

Outside Court Two – East Lancashire Magistrates Court

The doors slammed open.
Natalia exploded into the corridor like a bottle under pressure. Her coat flared behind her; her heels scuffed hard against the cheap vinyl floor. She didn't stop. Didn't look back. She just moved, fast, as if walking briskly could outpace the panic clawing up her throat.
Seth followed, jaw clenched, knuckles white around the strap of his bag. He was silent, but his shoulders were rigid with fury. Behind him, Izzy stumbled to keep up, her face pale and stunned, eyes blinking like she hadn't fully processed what she'd just witnessed.
"Remanded?" Natalia barked as they reached the bench by the window. "He's a child! He's our son, not some gangland psychopath!"
She wheeled around suddenly. "And where the hell is that

useless bastard?"

Cartwright appeared then, as if summoned by insult, his briefcase already half-open, sweat gleaming beneath his eyes. "Natalia... Mrs Overaugh... I can explain."

"No, I don't think you can," Seth said, stepping in front of his wife. His voice was low but thick with something dangerous.

"You said this would be a formality," Natalia spat. "You said it was just procedure. Just a holding charge."

"Well, yes, technically it is," Cartwright stammered, "but the magistrates..."

"They didn't trust a word you said!" Izzy snapped. "You were flipping through your notes like a Year Seven schoolboy who'd lost his homework!"

Cartwright tried to rally. "The prosecution came in heavier than expected. Their evidence presentation was... well, unusually forceful for a bail hearing."

Seth stepped forward. "You couldn't even find your place, Cartwright. You said Jonah 'regretted the confusion'. Are you trying to make him sound guilty?"

"I-I misspoke, yes, but..."

"You sweated your way through a bail application that might as well have been handwritten in crayon," Natalia said. "He's gone, Mr Cartwright. Do you understand that? They took him."

Cartwright's face coloured. "I assure you; I'll be pursuing the bail review as soon as possible."

"Don't," Seth said flatly. "Don't offer anything unless it's guaranteed. Just tell us what happens now."

The corridor felt like it was spinning. The cold light through the window turned everything sickly. Natalia dropped onto a nearby bench, her hands shaking. Izzy stood stiffly behind her; arms folded across her chest like she was holding herself together from the outside in.

Cartwright cleared his throat and straightened his glasses.
"Mr Overaugh has been remanded to Weatherby Young Offenders' Institute, as per standard protocol. It's a secure facility, but it's not prison in the adult sense. He'll be processed this afternoon, assigned a case officer, and placed under the standard twenty-four-hour monitoring for emotional distress."
"Emotional distress?" Natalia repeated hollowly. "He's never even been in a school detention. And now he's being locked up like a criminal."
"I understand your anger," Cartwright said carefully. "But Weatherby is designed for young offenders, not hardened criminals. It's staffed with educational teams, psychologists, social support…"
Seth cut in. "When can we see him?"
Cartwright looked down at his notes.
"There's a 72-hour intake window. They do an initial assessment, health screening, risk analysis. If all goes smoothly, you should be cleared for an in-person visit by Thursday afternoon. Late morning if the system moves quickly, but plan for Thursday."
Natalia's breath hitched. "Three days?"
"It's standard, I'm afraid. They'll allow a video call or

voicemail exchange sooner, if approved. But the first proper visit will require ID checks, transport arrangements, and an appointment time from their family liaison officer."
Izzy's voice came out hollow. "What will he be like in three days?"
Cartwright didn't answer.
He just adjusted his glasses again and looked anywhere but at them.
Seth nodded once. "Give us the contact. Their office. Whoever we call to get that arranged."
"Yes, of course," Cartwright said, scrambling through his file until he produced a pre-printed leaflet with the Weatherby intake protocol. "You'll need this. There's a phone number for the Family Liaison Officer, and I can send through his prisoner ID number once I receive it this afternoon."
"Prisoner? He's not a prisoner," Natalia snapped.
Cartwright winced. "Sorry - detainee. Young person on remand."
Natalia stood abruptly. "He's Jonah. My son. That's what he is."
The corridor seemed to fall still at that. Somewhere down the hallway, another courtroom door opened. Another case. Another disaster.
Seth put his hand on Natalia's back. She didn't move.
Izzy took the leaflet wordlessly and stuffed it into her coat pocket.
"Thursday," Seth repeated. "We see him Thursday."
Cartwright nodded.
And for once, said nothing more.

Chapter Twenty-Eight

Monday, 24th March 2025 – 10:58

En route to Wetherby Young Offenders' Institution

The van was quiet.
Jonah sat in the back of the secure transport vehicle, flanked by two officers he hadn't learned the names of. Not that it mattered. They hadn't spoken since they fastened his seatbelt. No words. Just movement.
The glass divider between the front and rear was smeared with fingerprints. The windows were frosted at the edges, muting the outside world. Beyond them, trees blurred past.
He couldn't stop shaking.
His fingers tapped against his knees involuntarily, a soft, rapid rhythm that matched the hammer of his heart. It wasn't panic now. Panic was too sharp, too fast. This was something else. A deep, slow horror. A realisation that didn't arrive all at once, but in pieces, like sinking into cold water.
The court hearing had barely felt real.

He could still hear the magistrate's voice. Calm. Efficient. Emotionless.

"You will be remanded into custody."
He'd known it was possible. Probable, even. But nothing could have prepared him for the cold slam of the door behind him as they'd taken him down the corridor, away from his family, away from his name.
He'd glanced back just once and seen his mum's face.
She had reached out instinctively, but the glass between them had stolen even that.
Now he sat in silence, his head leaning against the cold interior wall of the van, watching the countryside rush past like a film reel he wasn't allowed to pause.
They passed fields. Sheep. A petrol station. A school.
A school.
He looked away.

Monday, 24th March 2025 – 13:12

Wetherby YOI – Reception and Processing
The van pulled into a secure gate compound surrounded by high fencing topped with coils of razor wire. It didn't look like a prison - not from the outside. No towers. No spotlighted fences. But it didn't need to. The oppression was in the silence.
Inside, the routine was clinical.
The guards didn't shout. But they didn't smile either. Everything was spoken in short sentences and clipped

instructions.

"Stand there."

"Face forward."

"Hands behind your back."

Jonah followed everything like a puppet. Not because he was obedient, but because doing something – anything - was easier than being left alone with his thoughts.

A female officer at the front desk read from a clipboard without looking up. "Jonah Overaugh. Date of birth, 12th November 2006. Transferred from East Lancs Magistrates Court. Remanded under Section 25 Youth Justice and Criminal Evidence Act 1999. Charges: Perverting the course of justice in relation to a missing persons case."

She looked up. "First time in custody?"

Jonah nodded numbly.

"Any self-harm risk?"

He didn't speak.

The officer looked to the guard beside him. "He flagged on intake paperwork. Family concerns noted. Full risk screening."

She turned to Jonah again. "You'll be processed, medically screened, then placed under twenty-four-hour assessment. No visitors or calls until clearance is granted. That'll be 72 hours minimum. You understand?"

He nodded again.

She softened slightly. "You'll get through this."

He didn't believe her.

They took everything.

Shoes. Hoodie. His watch. The cheap wristband Brendan had

made him at a festival last summer. They logged it all, tagged it, sealed it in a clear poly bag with a white label.

They gave him issue clothing. Grey joggers. Off-white shirt. Plastic slip-on shoes that didn't fit right.

Then they took his photo.

The flash startled him. He blinked in the glare and tried to lift his chin. But he looked broken, even to himself. Pale. Gaunt. Lips pressed so tight together it made his jaw ache.

After that came the medical.

A nurse ran through questions in a soft tone, trying to coax answers out of him.

"Any history of anxiety? Depression? Trouble sleeping?"

Yes. Yes. Last night. Every night.

"Are you eating okay?"

No.

"Have you ever tried to harm yourself?"

He paused.

"No."

"Do you feel like harming yourself now?"

He shook his head, but it wasn't convincing.

She marked something on the form and added a red sticker to the top corner. "Okay. You'll be monitored hourly. If you need help, press the call button in your room. Don't be afraid to use it, alright?"

He nodded.

They handed him a welcome pack.

It contained a rules sheet, a pen, a mini toothpaste tube, and a small bar of soap wrapped in cellophane that smelled faintly like hospital corridors.

Monday, 24th March 2025 – 15:38

First Night Centre, Cell 2A
The cell was clean.
That was the first thing he noticed.
Cold, but clean. Off-white walls, no sharp edges. The mattress was thin, rubber coated. The blanket was stiff and scratchy. The toilet was built into the wall, no seat. A shelf. A tiny window too high to see out of.
There were no bars. Just a steel door with a narrow observation panel.
Jonah sat on the edge of the bed, clutching the blanket like it might tether him to something. Anything.
He couldn't cry. Not yet. That would come later.
Right now, all he could do was think.
About Brendan.
About the lies.
About the cold air in the car when he'd waited all night alone.
About the bleach smell at home.
About the locked granny flat door.
About Izzy's expression when she first saw him that morning.
He wrapped his arms around his knees and rocked slightly.
He wondered if his dad had driven back in silence. If his mum had cried in the car.
He wondered yet again about where Brendan was.
He wondered if he'd made him disappear. Not with his hands, but by being too weak to stop the plan. By letting Brendan go in alone. By not running after him when he'd been gone

too long.

The silence in the room began to hum.

His thoughts spun faster.

He paced. Stopped. Paced again. He read the rules sheet without taking in a word.

He tried to lie down. Couldn't.

Sat again.

At some point, he pressed the call button, not because he needed anything, but because he needed to know someone was out there. Someone real. Someone who hadn't disappeared.

An officer appeared in the viewing panel a few minutes later. "You alright?"

Jonah nodded, quickly, forcing himself to sound stable.

"Just... wanted to ask about when I can talk to someone."

"You'll have your key worker assessment tomorrow," the officer said. "Family visits start after seventy-two hours. They'll call you. You'll get to speak to them soon."

Jonah nodded again.

But soon didn't feel like enough.

The hatch slid shut again.

The silence returned.

Jonah lay down, pulling the blanket over his shoulders like armour.

He faced the wall and shut his eyes.

He didn't sleep.

But he pretended to.

Because that was all he had left to do.

Chapter Twenty-Nine

Monday, 24th March 2025 – 22:03

The silence had teeth now.
It pressed into the corners of the house like smoke, curling around furniture, clinging to the walls. No one had spoken since they got back from court. No one had dared. But it had to give eventually. Something always did.
And when it did, it detonated.
"I can't believe you let them take him," Izzy spat, slamming her water glass onto the counter so hard it cracked. "You just sat there and watched it happen!"
Seth stood by the back door, coat still hanging from his shoulders. He turned slowly, eyes narrowed. "We didn't let them do anything, Izzy. They are magistrates, they decide what happens not us."
"You didn't stop it either, did you?" she shouted. "You didn't stand up, didn't say a word, just let that useless solicitor fumble and fold and now… now he's gone."
Natalia, still seated at the kitchen table, looked up slowly.

"Izzy, we're trying. The bail application..."

"Don't," Izzy cut in. "Don't act like everything is under control. It's not. You both know what's going on. You know what happened that night. And now Jonah's sitting in a concrete box while you two walk around pretending you're just the tired, heartbroken parents."

"Izzy-" Seth warned.

"No! He's there because of you!" she snapped, turning on him now. "And because... what? Because you killed someone and buried the evidence? Because you didn't want the police snooping around? You killed Brendan for God sakes!"

Seth took a step forward. "Watch your mouth."

"No!" Izzy shouted. "You killed someone, Dad. You didn't just stop him, you obliterated him. And now Jonah's paying for it because you covered it up!"

Seth's voice dropped into a growl. "He's paying for what that scumbag did. That man attacked you, Izzy. Supposedly Jonah's friend, he's eaten at our table! Or have you forgotten that? It's not like we simply thought 'Oh let's kill Brendan'. No, he broke in, he came upstairs, into OUR sleeping area, OUR home and he attacked you!

"Have you thought about what that little scumbag might have done to you if me and your Mum weren't here? No, I don't think you did... well let me be very, very clear. The police can come and arrest people and lock them away, but they CANNOT un-rape you!"

"Don't twist this into you being a superhero," she snapped. "You didn't stop him. You destroyed him."

Seth's eyes flashed. "He deserved to be destroyed. He put his hands on my daughter and my wife. What was I supposed to do? Give him a cuddle and ask nicely?"

"That's not the point!" Izzy screamed, tears burning. "You didn't stop. You didn't even try. You went on and on like you were possessed. Like it was some sick release."

Natalia finally stood. "Enough."

But Izzy wouldn't stop. "Jonah is in custody. In a cell. And you're here burning garden waste and pretending this is normal. You think that's okay? You think he's just going to be fine?"

"I don't think it's okay," Natalia said firmly. "None of this is okay."

Seth threw his coat onto the back of a chair, his voice rising. "The only person to blame is the bastard in the ground! If he hadn't broken in, hadn't laid a finger on you two, none of this would've happened. And none of you have mentioned that Jonah needs to explain something here. Why was he waiting in Brendan's bloody car for five hours? Our son, our OWN SON drove him here... what the fuck is that about?"

"And you think murdering Brendan fixes it?" Izzy shouted. "You think that makes us better than him?"

"I did what any father would've done," Seth growled.

Natalia turned sharply. "No, you didn't."

Seth froze.

Natalia's voice was quieter now, but razor-sharp. "You didn't do what any father would've done. You went further. We both did. And don't stand there pretending it was all instinct. That wasn't just protection. That was something else and we both know it."

Seth stared at her. "So now you're blaming me?"

Natalia stepped closer. "I'm blaming both of us. But don't stand there and act like the knight in shining armour, you lost control."

Seth's voice dropped to a bitter low. "You think I don't remember? You weren't exactly playing patty-cake with him, Nat."

The words hit like a slap.

The room fell dead quiet.

Izzy stepped back, as if physically recoiling from the space between them.

Natalia's jaw set. "Don't you dare use that against me. I didn't ask to be dragged into that fight. I reacted. You? You enjoyed it."

Seth laughed bitterly. "You have no idea what went through my head. None."

"Then talk to me!" Natalia snapped. "Because all I see is a man who turned a self-defence incident into a massacre and now expects us all to pretend it was totally justified."

"I didn't have a choice!" Seth shouted.

"You had plenty of choices," Natalia hissed. "You chose rage. You chose to pick up that statue."

Seth went still.

Izzy frowned. "What does the statue have to do with anything?"

Neither of them answered.

The silence that followed was loaded.

Finally, Izzy grabbed her coat from the banister.

"Where are you going?" Natalia asked, her voice cracking.

"I don't know," Izzy replied. "Out. I can't stay in this house right now."

"Wait... Izzy..."

But she was already out the door, slamming it behind her with a violence that echoed through the stone walls.

Seth stood motionless, eyes fixed on the door.

Natalia sat back down, her arms crossed tightly over her chest, like she was holding herself together one more time before she fell apart.

Outside, the wind picked up.

Somewhere in the distance, a low groan rolled through the trees near the shed.

Neither of them spoke.

They just sat there, surrounded by silence and the ghosts they'd made together.

Chapter Thirty

Tuesday, 25th March 2025 – 09:02

Moorside House – Kitchen

The house was quiet again.
Not the quiet that brought peace. The kind that held its breath.
Natalia stood at the kitchen island, phone in hand, staring at the printed leaflet Cartwright had given her the day before. The header read:

'Youth Custody Visitation Protocol – Wetherby YOI'

It was written in bullet points. As if visiting your son in custody was no different than booking a dentist appointment.
She traced the number on the page with her finger.
Seth entered from the hallway, half-dressed, shirt unbuttoned, mug of black coffee steaming in his grip. He looked like he'd aged ten years overnight.

"Have you called?" he asked.

"Not yet."

"Why not?"

She didn't answer. Instead, she drew in a breath and dialled. The line rang. Once. Twice. A click, then a smooth female voice: "You have reached Wetherby Young Offenders' Institution. For family liaison services, press one…"

Natalia pressed one.

Another ring.

Then a voice answered. Clear, warm and calm.

"Family liaison, Wetherby speaking."

"Hi," Natalia said. "My name is Natalia Overaugh. My son Jonah Overaugh was remanded yesterday. We were told we can speak to someone about arranging a visit."

"One moment while I pull up the record… okay, yes, Jonah Overaugh. Intake confirmed Monday, 13:22. He's in the First Night Centre under observation. No red flags noted so far. He'll have his keyworker allocation by this afternoon."

Natalia's chest loosened a fraction. "That's good."

"We operate on a seventy-two-hour clearance window from point of intake. That means the earliest in-person visitation slot would be Thursday, 27th March, from 13:00 onwards."

Seth mouthed "Thursday" and nodded grimly.

"Right," Natalia said. "So, we book that through you?"

"You do. I can reserve a provisional slot for two named adults. Up to three people can attend, but we'll need full names, photo ID, and consent on record. Is he expecting you?"

Natalia blinked. "What?"

"Has he submitted your names for his approved list yet?"

"No... I don't know. I assume..."

"It's okay," the woman said gently. "We'll work around it. He'll meet with his case officer today. That form will be completed. For now, we'll hold a 13:30 visit for two on Thursday. Does that work?"

"Yes. Thank you."

"Names?"

"Natalia and Seth Overaugh."

"Confirmed. We'll call you Wednesday evening to reconfirm once he's officially signed off. You'll receive arrival protocols and ID check guidance by text."

"Okay."

"Anything else I can help with?"

Natalia's throat tightened. "Is he okay?"

A pause.

"Emotionally, or physically?"

"Both."

There was a kindness in the woman's voice now. "He's quiet. But compliant. He pressed the call button a few times last night, just to ask questions, mostly. That's usually a sign of someone looking for grounding. That's good. He hasn't been flagged as high risk."

Natalia closed her eyes. "Thank you."

They ended the call. She set the phone down slowly.

Seth leaned back against the counter. "Thursday then."

Natalia nodded. "13:30."

"Three days," he muttered.

"Two and a half," she replied.

He drained the last of his coffee and set the mug down harder than necessary. "That's still two and a half nights in a cell for something he didn't do."

She rubbed her temples. "He did lie to the police, Seth."

"And so did we," he said, voice sharp. "Only difference is, we did it with bleach and bin bags and didn't get caught."

She didn't argue. Couldn't.

He paced for a moment, then stopped. "Do you think he's scared?"

"Yes," she said. "More than we'll ever know."

Izzy entered the kitchen quietly, hoodie zipped to her throat, face unreadable. "Did you book it?"

"Thursday. One-thirty," Natalia said.

"Can I come?"

Seth looked at her. "Two people max. We'll rotate. First visit's just us."

Izzy nodded. "I want to see him, Dad. Before that place breaks him."

Seth didn't reply.

He just walked over to the sink and turned on the tap, staring at the stream of water like it might wash away what they'd done.

The remainder of the day passed quietly. No one said much. There were no more arguments, no further plans. Just movement. The quiet routines of survival. Natalia cleaned surfaces that didn't need cleaning. Seth chopped wood he didn't need to burn. Izzy sat at the kitchen table with her headphones in, sketching in her pad but drawing the same eye again and again.

The house remained still.

Even Lydia seemed subdued, curling in corners instead of following at heels.
By nine-thirty, Natalia stood and announced, "I'm going up."
Seth followed soon after, and Izzy not long after that. No goodnights. No reassurances. Just three people retreating to their separate corners, carrying with them the weight of the boy they couldn't reach.

Upstairs, the lights dimmed room by room. The familiar creaks of the house settled into a rhythm. Natalia lay curled on her side, staring at the wall. Seth lay flat on his back; hands folded across his chest. Izzy tucked the blanket under her chin and turned her face to the window.
At Wetherby, Jonah had done the same.
In his too-thin blanket, on his rubber mattress, with the flickering security light pulsing in the corner of his cell, he closed his eyes.
And like the rest of them, he drifted toward sleep.
Unaware that this time, they wouldn't be dreaming alone.

The dream did not come fast this time

It crept. Folded them in. One by one.
Jonah stirred first. He was running - again. But this time, not alone. Not frightened. Not in a car, or a cell. He was standing still, knee-deep in tall grass, the wind humming through it like a distant chant.

The field rolled out before him, silver in the moonlight. Moorside House rose on the hill beyond, its stone glistening wet, windows black and watching. The air tasted old, like soil and rot and something metallic.
He turned, confused.
And saw Izzy.
She stood across the field from him, half-lit, her hoodie stirring in the breeze. She looked younger here. Barefoot. Pale. Her eyes wide with realisation.
Their gazes locked.
"You're here too?" she asked, though her voice didn't carry across the distance. It arrived inside his head like thought.
"I think so, I think we're all here," Jonah replied.
Natalia stepped out from the hedgerow to his right, brushing long grass from her coat. She was barefoot too. Her hair loose. Her face drawn in quiet horror.
"What is this?" she said aloud.
"I don't know," Jonah said. "But it's real. Isn't it?"
Before anyone could answer, the wind shifted.

From the tree line, something moved.
A little girl - no more than eight- bolted across the field in a white nightgown, her bare feet silent in the grass. Her golden hair flew like silk behind her. Her breath came in high, gasping sobs.
Natalia inhaled sharply. "It's her."
"Lottie," Izzy whispered.
Jonah watched in numb awe as the girl tore through the grass, passing within feet of him. But she didn't look. Didn't stop.

She was running from something.
They all turned at once.
From the far edge of the field, a figure emerged.
Long black coat. Wide-brimmed hat. The outline flickered; sometimes clear, sometimes smudged, like the world itself wasn't sure it wanted him there.
But he kept coming.
And this time, they all saw it at once.
"Seth," Natalia whispered. Her voice trembled. "Oh my God. It's Seth."
"No," Izzy said. "It's him. The other one."
Jonah staggered backward. "You've seen him too?"
"Yes," The voice in their heads heard.
They all turned again.
Seth was stood by their side, breathing hard, eyes wide. He wasn't the man in the coat, thank the Lord. Not here. Not now. But he remembered. He felt it. He was watching it happen again, from the outside, and it was tearing him apart.
They all remembered.
"Who is he?" Natalia asked.
Seth didn't answer.
Just like before the figure surged forward.
The girl stumbled.
The field tilted, just slightly.
Jonah and Izzy both tried to run to her. But their feet sank into the ground, like the grass had turned to glue. Natalia shouted Lottie's name, but the wind swallowed the sound.
Seth watched it all, frozen in place, heart hammering.

"No," he said. "Please, not again."

But it was already happening.

The large green front door of Moorside House flew open with a loud bang, the sound reverberating across the open field. They switched focus to the house; the deep olive-green box frame vehicle was still idling at the side with the rear doors open as usual.

But this time a woman, no more than thirty years of age, burst out into the morning light in a storm of frantic movement. Her breath caught in the cold air as she stumbled forward onto the stone step, eyes scanning the horizon with wide, glassy panic.

She was dressed in 1940s garb; elegant yet practical. A calf-length A-line wool skirt billowed around her legs; the deep navy fabric creased from kneeling or pacing. Her blouse was ivory silk; its rounded collar fastened with a mother-of-pearl brooch that caught the light like a glint of warning. Over it, she wore a belted tweed overcoat tailored tightly at the waist, the shoulders structured, the cuffs slightly frayed with use.

Her stockings were rolled below the knee, revealing dust-caked ankles, and her sensible leather shoes, scuffed and unbuckled, slapped against the stone with every hurried step. Her chestnut hair was pinned in neat victory rolls, though strands had come loose in her panic, framing her face in chaotic curls. A single glove dangled from one hand, forgotten.

She stepped forward, trembling, then raised her voice... sharp, raw, and full of a mother's terror.
"LOTTIE!"
The word rang out across the field like a bell struck in grief. Her voice was frantic and piercing. Desperation carved into every syllable, just like the dreams; but this time, all four Overaughs could see her.
Jonah. Natalia. Izzy. Seth.
All of them watching.
She had barely cleared the stone step before another figure emerged into the grey morning light; older, heavier, slower. A matron, by look and movement. Thick ankles in black leather lace-up shoes clacked firmly on the slate. Her dress was sensible grey wool, buttoned all the way to the neck, with a black belt cinched so tight it folded her middle into two stiff halves. A white collar framed her throat, crisp and spotless despite the strain of the moment.
Her apron, starched and immaculately pressed, fluttered slightly in the rising breeze. On her head sat a small black felt hat, tipped just slightly forward, the netting barely touching her brow.
She followed the younger woman not with urgency, but with quiet insistence. Her steps were deliberate, her eyes sharp.
"Mrs Hawthorn!" she called, her voice tight and firm. "Please, come back inside."
The younger woman didn't stop.
The matron descended the step onto the gravel driveway, lifting her skirts just enough to move faster. "Mrs Hawthorn, please. It's for her own good."

There was no cruelty in her voice but no kindness either. Just a professional finality, the kind found in hospital corridors and locked wards. It was the voice of someone who believed order was compassion.

"She doesn't understand," the matron added, softer now. "You must trust the process."

"Lottie!" The younger woman cried, louder now, staggering down the gravel into the grass. "Lottie, come back!"

Her voice broke. She turned her head sharply toward the trees as if she could already feel the presence closing in. The wind lifted the hem of her skirt. Her coat flared.

And the house behind her loomed quietly, unchanged.

Just as it always had.

Just as it always would.

The man reached the girl in a burst of impossible speed. His arms wrapped around her, and she slammed into the grass… gone. The small scream died.

Seth's voice cut through the dream-space. "She can't see her," he said, staring at the young woman on the grass next to the driveway. "From where she's standing, the angle of the slope, the curvature of the field… she doesn't know." His eyes didn't leave the woman's figure, hands clenched at his sides.

"She's shouting for Lottie, begging, but she can't see below the ha-ha… where the wall builds up out of the sunken ditch. The girl is too small and that bastard has stayed too low for her to see him; He knows this place, the blind spots. She can't see what's already happening. She doesn't know her daughter's been taken."

He turned to the others - Natalia, Izzy, Jonah - his expression hollow. "She never saw it. Not once. She just... lost her."
And then... slowly, deliberately... as always, the man's head turned.
Towards them. All of them.
The figure looked first at Izzy, then at Jonah, then at Natalia. And finally, back at Seth.
The wide-brimmed hat tilted. The coat flared.
Then suddenly the coat began to retract, folding in on itself, warping and twisting as if made of smoke.
The face beneath began to form.
A glimpse of stubble.
A jawline.
Eyes.
And all of them saw the same thing.
Him. Twisted. Sharpened. Eyes burned through with something ancient, the face a darkened blur like a smudge on a TV screen.
The figure's obscured cheek bones lifted as he smiled. Not with joy, but with ownership.
And to his left, at the bottom left corner of the house now...
The statue.
Black basalt. Taller now. No longer still. It breathed with the rhythm of the dream. It was in the perfect position for a ringside seat.
Jonah turned to run.
Izzy screamed.
Natalia dropped to her knees.

Seth simply stood and stared, first at the man and then the statue.

The statue's eyes opened - blank, lightless voids - and fixed on them all.

And the voice came. Not spoken but felt. Felt through bone and nerve and soul.

"You're mine now."

And in that moment, from three different beds, in three different rooms, across two separate locations seventy-six miles apart, the Overaughs woke simultaneously with the same word on their lips.

Lottie.

Chapter Thirty-One

Wednesday, 26th March 2025 – 07:37

The kettle hadn't finished boiling when Izzy spoke.
"I saw you."
Seth turned from the sink, eyebrows pinched. "What?"
"In the dream," she said, sitting at the kitchen table, knees drawn up into her hoodie. "Last night. You were there. In the field. Watching it all."
Natalia froze with a jar of marmalade in her hand. Her voice was low when she replied.
"You weren't just watching, Izzy. You were in it."
Izzy's eyes flicked from her mother to her father. "So, we all saw the same thing?"
Seth leaned back against the counter and exhaled. "I think it's safe to assume we all saw it."
Natalia nodded. "I was in the field, near the hedgerow. I saw her, the girl. Lottie. I felt it again… that panic. That helplessness."
"I was across from Jonah," Izzy said quietly. "We looked at

each other. He was there too. I know it."

None of them had spoken when they first woke. The name Lottie had spilled from all three mouths like a cough, instinctual and involuntary. And now, gathered in the early morning light of the kitchen, there was no more denying it. They had shared the same dream.

Or something far worse.

"Do you think…" Natalia hesitated. "Do you think Jonah had it too?"

Seth didn't answer immediately. The kettle clicked off behind him. He poured boiling water into three mugs. None of them had asked for tea, but it gave his hands something to do.

"I think he did," he said finally. "And I think that means whatever this is… it's connected."

"To the house?" Izzy asked.

"To us," Natalia said. "To what we did. What we saw. What we're hiding."

Seth placed a mug in front of each of them. His shoulders were stiff, jaw set.

"I was him," he said quietly. "In the first dream. The man in the coat. Not just watching… inhabiting. I tackled her. I felt it. Every movement. Like it wasn't my body, but I knew exactly what it was doing."

Natalia looked up sharply. "You felt it?"

"Yes."

"Jesus…"

He took a slow sip of tea. "And now we've all seen it. We were all present. That wasn't just trauma. That wasn't guilt. That was a… a replay. Like a memory."

"A memory of what?" Izzy asked, voice trembling.

Natalia looked toward the snug. "Of here. Of this house."

Izzy followed her gaze. "So, who is she?"

"Lottie," Natalia said. "That's the only name we've got."

Seth's voice was low. "And the woman who ran out of the house, she was called Hawthorn. The matron shouted it. 'Mrs Hawthorn, it's for her own good'."

"I heard it too," Izzy said. "That woman wasn't just a stranger. She belonged here."

"I know the Hawthorns owned this house in the forties or fifties and they sold it on; James Hawthorn was a pilot in the war I think." Seth added.

"So, this is the past?" Natalia said. "We're seeing something that happened?"

"Or something that never stopped." Seth muttered.

They fell silent again.

The wind outside moaned softly through the chimney. Somewhere overhead, Lydia paced on the landing, claws clicking on hardwood.

Izzy leaned forward, elbows on the table. "Do you think the statue is causing it?"

Seth didn't respond immediately. When he did, he looked at Natalia. "Only me and your mother touched it, and we took it out of the house. It's in the shed."

"That's wrong," Izzy whispered. "I did touch it, when the creep pushed me into the sideboard initially, I went into all the ornaments and they fell off, that's how it landed on the floor."

Natalia shivered. "It was in the dream. Same place. Same

presence. I didn't want to throw it away at first, but since it's been in the shed, I've felt loads better"

"It watched," Izzy said. "It always watches; I can feel it"

Seth pinched the bridge of his nose. "If Jonah had that dream last night too, and woke up alone in a cell…"

"He'll be terrified," Natalia finished for him. "And more alone than ever. We need to know if and when he touched it."

They sat in that heavy silence for a long time, tea cooling in their mugs, the shadows stretching slowly across the floor. Finally, Seth broke it.

"Right, I'm not having us chasing shadows and getting the heebie-jeebies over a bloody dream and an inanimate object. That's just insane!"

"As insane as caving your son's friends head in with it and then keeping it in the shed?" Izzy snapped.

Seth winced.

Natalia stiffened. "Let's get rid of it… right now, why we didn't do that in the first place is beyond me. My money is on it's trying to protect itself."

Seth stood and walked to the back door "We'll do one better than that, we'll smash it to bits then throw it in the canal. Let's see it protect itself against that!"

Natalia and Izzy followed Seth outside to the shed. Its door groaned open under Seth's hand, the old hinges complaining as the morning light spilled across the cluttered floor. Dust motes danced in the beam from the kitchen window.

The statue was right where he'd left it; perched behind two tins of dried-out fence paint, wrapped in the same tea towel, its dark bulk hunched on the shelf like it had been waiting.

Seth didn't hesitate this time. He reached in and grabbed it with both hands. It was heavy, heavier than it looked, but he carried it out without comment, eyes forward.

Natalia and Izzy stood just outside the door, arms crossed, tension simmering in their shoulders.

Seth set the statue down in the middle of the gravel beside the old fire pit. "Right," he muttered. "Let's end this."

He walked briskly to the far side of the shed, returning moments later with his sledgehammer - a thick-handled, well-worn thing he'd used to demolish the brick steps at the front of the house two summers ago.

He rolled his shoulders once, then lifted the hammer high above his head and brought it down with a thunderous crack.

The sound split the air.

The gravel sprayed slightly under the impact.

But the statue didn't budge.

No fracture. No chip. No mark.

The hammer had bounced off... recoiled, like it had hit steel wrapped in rubber.

Seth stepped back, blinking. "You're joking."

He gritted his teeth, steadied his grip, and tried again. Harder. Another strike. Another ringing crack.

The sledgehammer flew from his hands this time, the force of the rebound pulling it away as if it had struck an invisible wall. It landed three feet away in the grass with a dull thud.

Natalia covered her mouth.

Izzy whispered, "That's not possible..."

Seth walked over, picked up the hammer again; more slowly this time. "It's just stone," he muttered. "It has to be."

He tried a third time. Nothing.

Not even a scuff.

Breathing hard now, he threw the hammer aside and disappeared into the shed once more. Natalia and Izzy exchanged a glance, half fear, half disbelief.

When Seth returned, he was carrying his angle grinder.

"Right," he said grimly. "Let's see how you handle this."

He plugged it into the extension cord that fed out from the outside sockets in the garden, checked the blade, and ignited the motor. The air filled with its piercing scream as the blade spun to life.

He lowered it to the surface of the statue, carefully, precisely.

And met resistance instantly.

The moment the blade kissed the basalt, it threw sparks. Not the kind you expect. No shower of dust or shard, just sudden light. The whine of the tool deepened into a pained growl. The vibration in Seth's hands changed.

He tried again, pressing harder.

The blade dulled in seconds.

The edge glowed faintly red before the motor groaned and cut out entirely.

Seth stepped back, swearing under his breath. The grinder hissed with the smell of burnt metal and friction.

Izzy knelt beside the statue and ran a hand over its surface.

Still cool. Still smooth.

Still perfect.

Except…

"There," she whispered. "The scratches. Still there."

Seth crouched beside her.

The three faint diagonal lines across the base were shallow but clear. Not cracks... scratches. Deliberate. Uneven. Like they'd been made with something sharp and specific.

"If this thing's indestructible," Natalia said from behind them, "then how did those get there?"

Seth didn't answer. He just stared at them.

Izzy looked up. "So, we can't destroy it. What do we do?"

Seth ran a hand down his face, streaking sweat and disbelief into the creases at his jaw. "Right. That's it. If it can't be smashed, and it can't be cut, then we throw it in the canal. Tonight. No-one will know."

Natalia hesitated. "We can't."

Seth turned toward her. "Why not? You said it yourself; you don't want it near the house."

"I don't," she snapped, "but throwing it away doesn't make it disappear. If someone finds it - fishermen, kids, anyone - and it ever gets traced back here..."

"To us?" he said, incredulous. "It's just a lump of stone."

"It's not just a lump of stone," she replied. "Not anymore. There are records. Inventory lists. Old estate photos. That thing's in half the auction brochures they handed us when we bought this place. It's part of the bloody grade 2 listing! If it turns up somewhere... it's tied to Moorside. Which means it's tied to us and that gives the finder cart blanche to ask questions and poke around in places we don't want anyone poking in, and let's face it that bloody thing has a way of drawing people in, just like us. Until we figure out how to destroy it we need to make sure we know where it is whilst keeping it away from prying eyes."

Izzy, arms folded tightly, nodded. "She's right. We can't just dump it. There's a trail and obviously we can't trust something like this to stay buried."

Seth looked at the statue again; dull, silent, still utterly untouched despite everything. "So what? We just keep it?"

"I don't know," Natalia said. "But we don't risk someone else waking it up."

Then came the voice.

"Woo-hoo, everything alright over there?"

They turned.

Mary Ashcroft stood at the edge of the adjoining field about 20 metres away, her mug of tea steaming in the cool morning air. Her waxed jacket was already flecked with straw. The collie at her heel barked once before dropping to sit and sniff the air to see if it could locate Lydia.

Seth straightened immediately, stepping in front of the statue. "Morning, Mary!"

Mary tilted her head, amused. "Bit early for heavy metal. Heard the grinder going from the barn."

Natalia wiped her hands down her jeans and smiled faintly. "Hinge on the shed door's rusted through. Seth got impatient."

"Well, he's got the whole valley up," Mary said with a grin. "Just as well I was already feeding the stock."

Izzy stepped forward, trying to look casual. "Sorry, Mary. We'll keep it down."

Mary's eyes drifted to the left then right. "What's that, then?

Looks like one of them old Army crates."
Seths expression dropped. Fuck, the crate!
They had been meeting themselves forwards going backwards in recent days and the small crate they had found had completely slipped his mind.
They had put it behind the logs to deal with later so no-one could see it from the driveway, but from Mary's field it was very much visible.
Seth forced a chuckle. "Ah, it's just an old crate I found in the shed, when I was cleaning it out, I used it as a step to get to the top of the wood pile.
"Ah, I see," Mary said.
"Mr Little Legs over here always need a step ladder," Natalia threw in quickly.
Mary took another sip of tea. "Well, I won't keep you. Just checking the racket wasn't someone chopping off a hand or something. Don't burn the place down."
Seth smiled. "We'll try not to."
Izzy whispered under her breath so only her parents could hear. *"Don't worry Mary, we saw the arms off round these parts."*
Nat nudged her in the ribs and whispered her to be quiet.
Natalia then waved a good neighbourly hand. "Thanks Mary: don't worry we won't."
With a tip of her head and a low whistle to the dog, Mary turned back across the field. The collie trotted after her, glancing back once before vanishing into the tall grass.

The silence returned.

But not the stillness.

Seth turned back to the statue. "Right. Back in the shed and we'll deal with this later, when we've had time to think. Izzy- grab that crate for me."

Izzy huffed and then complied.

They didn't speak again until both crate and statue were tucked away in the shed.

Chapter Thirty-Two

Thursday, 27th March 2025 – 07:56

Today was the day.
Natalia sat at the kitchen table, still in her dressing gown, one hand wrapped around a mug of untouched tea, the other scrolling through her phone. Her face had stiffened into something neutral. Expressionless, but not at peace.
"I thought you didn't use social," Seth said, walking in with his laptop tucked under his arm.
"I don't," she said flatly. "Just Pinterest. Recipes. Garden stuff. But I've still got Facebook and Insta for family pictures and memories. I forgot they were even logged in."
She turned the screen toward him.
A photo of Brendan from a few months ago, sitting on the bonnet of his car, laughing, a can of energy drink in hand, had been reshared by someone neither of them knew.
The caption read:

'Still no word on Brendan Hughes. Last seen with Jonah

Overaugh. Something doesn't add up'

Below it:
#FindBrendan #JusticeForBrendan #JonahKnows
Seth's mouth set into a thin line.
"Is that public?" he asked.
"Of course it is," Natalia said bitterly. "It's already been shared sixty-seven times. And look at the comments. Even Jane is piling on."
He didn't want to. She scrolled anyway.
"That Jonah kid always seemed off to me."
"Where there's smoke…"
"Check the parents too. Bet they're covering."
"Creepiest house in the village - figures."
"That last one was from Gary at the pub. The feckless dim wit, I never did like him." She finally sipped her tea.
Izzy entered, her phone in hand, earbuds still looped around her neck. "Mum, my DMs are full of people asking if Jonah ever hurt animals or if he was bullied in school. Like they're building a bloody Netflix documentary."
"Jesus," Seth muttered. He set the laptop down on the table and rubbed his forehead. "I knew this would happen."
"What do we do?" Natalia asked.
Seth clicked into gear. "We screenshot everything. Every comment, every message, every repost. If they're suggesting Jonah's dangerous, or that we're involved we keep the record. Document the timestamps. Tag the usernames. Then email it all to me."
"I've already got a folder," Izzy said. "Dozens. Most of them

are burner accounts or profiles with ten followers and a dog photo."

"Doesn't matter," Seth said. "We hand it over to McIntyre and let the police decide what's worth tracing. If nothing else, we've got it logged."

Natalia's thumb hovered over her screen. "Should I deactivate the accounts?"

Seth shook his head. "Not yet. If it escalates, we'll take them down. But right now, we need to be able to see what's being said."

"I can't believe people are treating it like a true-crime puzzle," Izzy said. "They're acting like it's entertainment, like it's 'The Vanishing of Brendan' or something"

Seth glanced at the clock. "And we've got less than three hours before we walk into that facility and see our son for the first time in nearly a week. So, we don't engage. We don't post. We just document and stay quiet."

Natalia stood and pushed her mug aside, barely touched.

"I'll shower," she said. "We should leave by twelve. I don't want to be late. I've already sent an email to college for Izzy being off this week. Have you sorted work Seth?"

He nodded. "Yeah, it's fine, Dave is covering. Don't worry We'll be ready."

But no one felt ready.

Not for Wetherby.

Not for Jonah.

And certainly not for the world outside their front door that had already started making up its mind.

They left Moorside in silence.

Seth drove the Audi A4. Natalia sat beside him, her coat zipped to the chin, hands clenched in her lap. Izzy curled into the back seat, hood up, forehead against the glass. None of them spoke for the first ten miles.

The roads through Accrington were narrow and familiar: Spring Hill, Plantation Street, then down to the A680, winding past old mills and clusters of half-abandoned shops. Everything looked washed-out in the early afternoon light. As they turned onto the A56 southbound, the car finally picked up speed.

At Junction eight, Seth merged them onto the M65 heading east. The landscape opened up briefly. Low hills and fields blurring past in quiet resignation.

The M65 soon fed them onto the M66 southbound, taking them around Bury, through the outskirts of Heywood and Middleton. Every so often a blue sign flashed overhead - 'Leeds (M62 East)' - reminding them they were heading further from the world they knew.

At the interchange near Simister Island, Seth took the slip for the M62 eastbound. The air seemed to change there; flatter, windier. The traffic thickened briefly around Rochdale, then loosened again as they passed Huddersfield and into West Yorkshire proper.

Izzy didn't lift her head.

Seth exited onto the M1 northbound, the sky stretching wide and overcast above them. The signs counted down like a clock. Wetherby: 25 miles, then 20, then 15.

Natalia reached for his hand. He let her hold it.
Finally, they took the exit for Wetherby and followed the A-road, a quiet stretch that led them through the edges of the town; a place that looked too clean, too quiet to house what awaited them. Clearly, this town was getting grant funding from somewhere.
The Young Offenders' Institution was signposted discreetly, just past a roundabout with a garden centre and a cluster of low brick homes. The facility itself sat behind a high fence, modern and unimposing, but no less intimidating for its politeness.
Seth turned into the visitor car park and killed the engine.
No one moved.
They just stared at the entrance.
Not knowing what they'd see inside.
Hoping Jonah would still be the same and fearing that he wouldn't.

Chapter Thirty-Three

Thursday, 27th March 2025 – 13:24

The reception building at Wetherby YOI was squat and institutional, all clean lines and damp-proof render, its friendliness only skin-deep. Natalia stood first at the check-in desk, handing over their printed confirmation and IDs.
The officer behind the glass, a woman in her early fifties with clipped hair and a neutral expression, glanced at the forms and scanned the IDs one at a time.
"Two visitors pre-cleared for today: Natalia and Seth Overaugh," she said flatly, then looked up at Izzy. "I don't have an Isabel Overaugh listed."
"She's our daughter," Natalia said gently. "We were told only two at a time. She wasn't on the first rotation, but we couldn't leave her at home on her own."
The woman nodded. "That's correct. Visitation lists are normally locked 24 hours before the session. But…"
She paused, tapping her keyboard.
"…this is a first visit. The system notes it's flagged for

compassionate handling. If you're all here and he's asked to see family, we can make a one-time exception."

Natalia's shoulders relaxed. "Thank you."

"I'll need verbal confirmation from your son's side once he's brought in," the woman added. "If he agrees to all three, we'll proceed. But going forward, it'll be two at a time, as per policy."

"Understood," Seth said.

They completed the rest of the check-in procedure quickly; emptying pockets, passing through the scanner, locking up their belongings in assigned lockers. The process was quiet and efficient, but every metal beep and clink of a latch sounded louder than it should have.

A young officer in a blue YOI uniform, his name tag reading Officer Reeve, stepped through the internal security door and waved them forward.

"Overaugh family?" he asked. "Come through. Jonah's prepped and waiting. We'll confirm the guest list when we get to the visit suite."

They followed him down a long, clean corridor under the dull thrum of the overhead fluorescents. The doors were steel and smooth, the windows thin and wired. The whole building felt like it had been designed to be forgotten.

"This is the visit wing," Reeve explained. "Conversations are supervised but not monitored unless there's risk flagged. No physical contact at the start or end. Forty-minute limit. If you need to end early, use the red buzzer."

They stopped outside a plain door marked 'VISIT ROOM 3'.

Reeve tapped his earpiece. "Room three, Overaugh family, requesting tri-pass... yes, confirmed, Jonah has approved the third party."

He turned back to them with a nod. "Alright. You're all clear. Table six, in the far corner."

The door opened.

The room beyond was quiet. A few other families sat at spaced-out tables, speaking in hushed tones. Everything felt muted as if someone had dialled down the colour and volume of the world.

Jonah entered from a side door less than a minute later, escorted by a silent staff member in grey.

He looked thinner than Seth remembered. Paler. His hair was unwashed and flat. His clothes were standard issue: grey joggers, plain sweatshirt, white trainers. He shuffled in, arms folded tightly and froze when he saw them.

Izzy smiled first.

Then Jonah smiled: small, exhausted, but real.

They sat.

Seth reached for words and found none.

Natalia blinked too much but didn't cry.

Izzy leaned in. "Told you we'd come."

Jonah looked at each of them, his hands trembling slightly in his lap.

"I didn't think they'd let you all in."

"They nearly didn't," Natalia said gently. "But they made an exception. Just this once."

"I'm glad," Jonah whispered.

And for the first time in days, he didn't feel like a number.

Chapter Thirty-Four

Thursday, 27th March 2025 – 13:32

Wetherby YOI – Visit Room Three

They sat around the bolted metal table, a pitcher of lukewarm water and four plastic cups between them. Somewhere behind them, another family murmured and sniffled over their own unravelling.
Seth shifted in his chair and leaned forward, arms on the table.
"Alright, son," he said, voice low but firm. "You've had a few days to think. So, I'm going to ask you something, and I want a straight answer."
Jonah looked up, cautious.
Seth met his eyes. "What were you and Brendan doing at Moorside Industrial Estate for five hours that night?"
There it was.
Jonah blinked. "That's your question?"
Seth frowned. "Yes."

"Really? You're starting with that? You're not going to ask where Brendan is?" Jonah said, his tone sharper now. "Not going to ask if he's alive? Or if I've heard from him? You're going to start with that?"

Natalia touched Jonah's arm gently. "He's asking because it matters, love. The police already know where you were. They're building timelines."

Before Jonah could respond, a voice snapped from across the room.

"No contact."

The supervisor, broad-shouldered, seated near the far wall, was already on his feet. His tone wasn't aggressive, but it carried weight.

"All visitors... hands on the table... no physical contact during conversation."

Natalia pulled her hand back immediately, her face flushing as she nodded.

"Sorry," she said quietly, palms now flat on the table.

Jonah glanced at the officer, then back to his family, jaw clenched.

Jonah pulled forward slightly. "I know what they're building."

Izzy leaned forward, her voice soft. "Jonah... five hours is a long time."

Jonah's jaw clenched again. "We were talking. Arguing. Planning stupid stuff. Hanging around."

"In the dark? In the cold?" Seth asked. "No phones. No heater. No music. Just sitting in the car like ghosts?"

Jonah exhaled sharply. "We were trying not to get caught on CCTV, alright?"

That drew silence.

Natalia looked startled. "Caught doing what?"

Jonah's eyes burned with frustration. "Nothing that matters anymore. Brendan had this idea; he kept going on about how your watch insurance was renewed. Said it'd be a victimless job. 'Take a few, claim them back. Win-win.' His words, not mine."

Seth stared at him. "So, you were going to rob your own house. You were going to rob me?"

"No," Jonah snapped. "He was. I was just the idiot who left the flat door open and sat in the car like a coward while he did it."

Izzy covered her mouth.

Natalia whispered, "Jesus, Jonah..."

"Yeah," he said. "Welcome to my week."

Seth's voice had dropped. "So, he went in. You waited. And then what?"

"He didn't come back," Jonah said. "I waited. I waited until five in the morning, and he never came back."

"And you didn't tell us?" Natalia asked, her voice breaking.

"What was I supposed to say?" Jonah hissed. "That Brendan Hughes vanished whilst trying to rob our house and I was the getaway driver?"

"You lied to the police," Seth said. "You lied to us."

Jonah slammed his fist on the table, hard enough to rattle the water jug. "And you still haven't answered my question!"

"Take it easy," the supervisor called over, not shouting, but firm. "Keep your hands on the table and voices down."

Jonah nodded stiffly, exhaling through his nose as he pressed

both palms flat against the metal surface.
"Sorry," he muttered without looking up.
Everyone froze.
Jonah's voice was shaking now. "Why did you ask about the five hours in the car, Dad? Why that first? Why not 'Where's Brendan?' or 'Did something happen?' Why skip all that and jump straight to the gap? Not to mention you're all acting weird."
Seth opened his mouth. Closed it again.
"Do you guys know something?" Jonah asked, quieter now. "Because something happened inside that house after I left?"
Natalia's face had gone pale.
"I came home," Jonah said. "I smelt the bleach. I saw your hands Dad. I saw Izzy not talking and the granny flat door mysteriously locked when I know I left it open, and no one goes in that part of the house."
He looked from one to the other.
"I kept my mouth shut because I thought Brendan messed up. Got caught. But now? After the dreams? After that thing in the dream. Don't you dare look at me like I'm the only one hiding something."
Natalia's eyes filled with tears.
Izzy stared at the table.
Seth said nothing.
Jonah leaned back in his chair, eyes red but dry.
"So go on," he muttered. "Ask your questions. I'll give you straight answers now. But after this... I expect the same in return."
The silence between them felt like it stretched for a lifetime.

Finally, Natalia spoke. Quiet, measured, her voice barely holding together.

"Jonah... did you see anything that night? After Brendan left the car?"

Jonah frowned. "No. I stayed put. I kept looking up the canal path, waiting to see his silhouette. I thought maybe he got caught by a motion light, or your car alarm, or... I don't know, something." He paused, then added, "But he never came. Not even a sound. It was like he vanished."

Seth leaned forward again, eyes dark. "Did he have anything on him? Tools? Bag?"

Jonah shook his head. "No. He said he didn't need them. 'In and out,' remember? That was the whole point. Door already unlocked. No cameras."

Izzy finally spoke, her voice smaller now. "You were going to steal from Dad? You really are stupid, why didn't you just ask for money"

Jonah winced. "I didn't plan it. Brendan... he made it sound like it didn't matter. Like it wouldn't even be real and there is no way you'd give me money to go on a lads' bender."

"It is real," Seth said sharply. "We are real. Our family is not a fucking mark for you and your dipshit mates!"

Jonah snapped back. "I know that alright?"

Seth's fingers flexed on the table. Natalia touched his wrist gently, calming him. Her voice was soft but serious. "Jonah... we need to tell you something. And you're not going to like it."

Jonah looked at her carefully, reading her expression. "Is this about the statue? I keep seeing it in my dreams."

Natalia blinked. "Yes. But not just that."
Seth exhaled hard through his nose. "There was an intruder. The same night Brendan disappeared. Someone broke into the house. Came up the stairs. Attacked Izzy."
Jonah sat up straighter. "What?"
Izzy nodded slowly, swallowing hard. "He didn't say anything. He just attacked me." Her voice trembled. "I screamed. Mum came. So did Dad."
"And then what?" Jonah asked, already fearing the answer.
Natalia stared into her lap. "We... reacted. We defended ourselves. Seth... hit him. Hard. I did too."
Jonah's voice lowered. "With what?"
Seth didn't hesitate. "The statue."
Jonah's mouth went dry. "Wait, did you kill him?"
No one answered.
Which was answer enough.
Jonah went pale, he started to feel nauseous.
"Oh my God," Jonah whispered. "You killed him. And you didn't say anything?"
"He attacked your sister," Seth said, jaw tight. "We didn't plan this. We didn't want it. But it happened. And then..."
"And then you cleaned it up," Jonah cut in. "The bleach. The DVRs, your hand."
"We were trying to protect you," Natalia said quickly. "Protect Izzy."
Jonah stared at all three of them in disbelief. "So, while I was sitting in a freezing car thinking Brendan had been caught, you were doing what? Disposing of his body?"
The silence roared.

Seth leaned forward. "We don't know who he was. His face was unrecognisable. His clothes were... strange. Out of place."
Jonah shook his head. "His face was unrecognisable... What the fuck did you do to him? And then what... Did you bury him or something?"
Natalia looked solemn.
"Jesus Christ, where?" Jonah's eyes started to look frantic.
"Let's just say we won't be having marshmallows and fireworks on bonfire night this year." Izzy just couldn't help herself.
"Under the fire pit," Natalia confirmed after giving Izzy a dangerous looking side eye. "It was the only option."
"Not the only option," Jonah snapped. "Just the easiest one that didn't involve the police."
Izzy looked up, voice cracking. "We were scared, Jonah."
He sat back in his chair again, jaw twitching.
"And Brendan?"
No one answered.
Seth looked down.
"You don't think it was him," Jonah said slowly. "You know it was him."
"No," Natalia whispered. "We don't. We can't be sure. His face was too damaged. There was no ID. But..."
"But it makes too much sense," Jonah finished for her. "Same night. Same time. Brendan's plan. My friend."
Seth's voice was a low growl. "It wasn't your fault."
"Wasn't it?" Jonah said. "I bought into this madness."
"No," Natalia said firmly. "He made his own choices. If he cooked up the scheme, then it's on him."

They fell silent again, the four of them orbiting the truth, unable to pull away and too terrified to fall in.

Then Izzy whispered, "We're cursed."

Jonah looked at her. "What?"

Izzy's eyes were glassy. "We all had the dream, I take it? About Lottie. The girl. The house. The man."

Seth's face hardened. "The figure was me in my first dream."

Jonah didn't flinch. He simply nodded.

Natalia added, "But it wasn't you, Seth. Not really. It was something using you. Moving through you."

Jonah folded his arms slowly. "So... we're not just dealing with death. We're dealing with something worse."

Seth looked up. "The past."

"And the statue," Natalia said. "We tried to destroy it. We couldn't."

"Don't forget the dead body" Izzy interjected.

Jonah ran a hand down his face.

"Well," he said bitterly, "we're really in it now."

The low murmur of voices and the quiet rustle of plastic chairs was broken by the sharp voice of the supervising officer. "Time! That's forty minutes; visit's over. Hands where we can see them."

Chairs scraped against the floor as other families began to rise. Jonah didn't move at first. He just looked at them. At his mum, his dad and Izzy; as if he was trying to memorise their faces before they were taken away again. Then slowly, he stood. No one reached for a hug. No one dared. The rules were iron, and this moment was glass.

He gave the smallest nod, then turned as the officer opened the door behind him. And just like that, he was gone again; swallowed by the system, leaving silence in his place.

The walk back through the corridor was longer this time. The fluorescent lights still buzzed above them, casting their shadows against the pale walls as if even the building was trying to hold onto their guilt. No one spoke. The clicking of Izzy's boots echoed off the floor, the only sound accompanying them through the reinforced doors and back into reception. Natalia collected the locker keys. Seth signed them out with a hand that trembled just slightly as he pressed the pen to the form.

Outside, the cold felt sharper than before. They climbed into the car in silence. Seth drove. Natalia stared out of the passenger window, eyes fixed on nothing. Izzy sat in the back again, arms folded, jaw clenched, earbuds in but no music playing.

The motorway came and went in a blur of greys and greens, but none of them noticed the signs or the miles. Each was locked in their own loop: Jonah's voice, the things that had been said... and the truths they had the courage to share.

Chapter Thirty-Five

Friday, 28th March 2025 – 11:14

They had gone to bed the night before without a word. No debrief. No discussion. Just three heavy-footed climbs up the stairs and doors clicking shut.
The house had been quiet. Not the fragile kind of quiet that tiptoes around grief, but the thick, resigned kind that follows exhaustion. None of them had slept well; not after seeing Jonah's face, hearing his voice, or absorbing the weight of what they'd all admitted. Thankfully there was no dream to contend with.
Now, in the grey light of morning, they sat in the snug. Not together, not really. Just in proximity.
Natalia perched on the edge of the armchair with a half-drunk mug of tea gone cold. Seth stood near the window, arms crossed, watching nothing. Izzy was curled up on the floor cushions in the corner, knees tucked to her chest, phone in hand.
The only sound was the soft flicking of her thumb on the

screen and the occasional intake of breath.

"Still bad?" Natalia asked gently, though she already knew the answer.

Izzy didn't look up. "Worse. Some of them are making videos now."

Seth turned from the window. "Videos?"

"TikTok. Insta Reels. Someone pulled a picture of Jonah from Mum's Facebook and spliced it into one of those crime recap things. There's a voiceover. They're treating him like a bloody character."

Seth clenched his jaw. "Send me everything. Screenshots. Links. I want copies of the usernames too."

"I'm already saving them," Izzy said. "It's all in the same folder as before."

Seth walked over and crouched beside her. "Let me see."

Izzy handed him the phone. He scrolled through the messages. Some were vague, just hashtags and speculation, but others were vile. Direct. Accusatory.

One comment stood out:

"If Jonah's innocent, why does his sister look so smug?"

Seth handed the phone back, stood up and ran a hand over his face.

"Enough," he muttered. "I'm not letting this carry on."

He walked over to the sideboard, grabbed his phone, and began thumbing through his contacts.

Natalia looked over. "Who are you calling?"

"McIntyre," he said. "If they are keeping Jonah in custody, the least they can do is warn people off tearing his family apart online."

He tapped the name and hit call, pacing the room as it rang.

East Lancashire CID – Briefing Room Two

DC Sarah McIntyre sat at the edge of the plastic desk, coffee cup in hand, scrolling through a series of case notes on her tablet. Across from her, DS Hargreaves leaned against the filing cabinet with a folded copy of the local paper tucked under his arm.

"You seen this?" he asked, tapping the headline.
'Missing Teen Linked to Prominent Moorside Family'

McIntyre didn't look up. "Saw it last night. Amateur garbage. Full of speculation, no sourcing. And now we've got the whole family being dragged into it too. Public's getting restless."
Hargreaves snorted. "Restless is good. Restless makes people talk."
"Restless also gets lawyers involved," she muttered, setting the cup down. "The mum's been playing composed, but the dad? There's something off about him. He's too polished. Too careful."
"Seth Overaugh," Hargreaves said, testing the name like he was chewing on it. "Executive type. Corporate IT background. Likely knows how to manage a narrative."
McIntyre nodded. "Exactly. I don't trust that one inch. The kid lied, sure... but I think he's scared. I think the dad's the one doing the damage control."

"And the mother?"

"She's too close to it. Probably doesn't even realise how much she's covering for him."

Hargreaves stepped closer. "So, what's the play, then? We can't hold the boy much longer now."

"No," McIntyre said, lowering her voice. "But we don't have to let them off the hook either. We keep our options open. I've already logged a request for Jonah's bail conditions; tight ones. Home address lock-in. No contact with Hughes. Full monitoring."

Hargreaves raised an eyebrow. "And you're still not telling them?"

She looked at him. "Let them sweat. They've been playing us since day one. If they want answers, they can come and get them in person. There is a lot more to all this than meets the eye."

Just then, McIntyre's mobile rang on the desk beside her. She picked it up, glanced at the caller ID, and smirked.

"Well," she said dryly. "Mention the devil and he shall appear."

She answered, pressing the phone to her ear. "We thought you'd be in touch, Mr Overaugh."

"You could sound a bit less pleased about it," he replied.

"I'm not pleased, just unsurprised. What can I do for you?"

"My daughter's being harassed online. Jonah's name is plastered across half the internet. Izzy's had direct messages, tagged posts, even videos accusing her of covering something up. It's getting worse by the hour."

"We are aware of some of the online activity. Have you

documented it?"

"Yes. Screenshots, account handles, timestamps. We've archived everything."

"Good," she replied. "Email the evidence to me directly. I'll log it with our digital harm unit and flag it with the community protection team. Send it today."

"Done. I'll get it over within the hour."

There was a pause before Seth asked his question. "Is there any news? About Jonah?"

The response from McIntyre was delivered in level tones: "Yes. He'll be released on bail later this afternoon.

"You can collect him from Wetherby YOI once the paperwork's cleared. They'll contact you when he's ready. Should be sometime after three."

"So that's it? No explanation? You're just letting him out?"

"I'm not just doing anything, Mr Overaugh. Jonah's being released under strict bail conditions pending further investigation."

"Which you're not going to explain either, I take it?"

She responded sharply: "I'm retaining investigative control. That includes what is or isn't shared with you. For now, you'll be informed of the conditions in writing when you collect your son."

"You're playing games," Seth told her.

"No. I'm doing my job. And I suggest you start preparing to do yours. Jonah's going to need a lot more than silence when he walks out of that place."

There was a stiff period of silence before McIntyre enquired: "Anything else?"

"No."

"Then I'll expect your email shortly. Goodbye."

Seth ended the call and let the phone drop to his thigh, staring at nothing. His jaw was tight, a tendon twitching along his cheek.

Natalia was already on her feet. "Well?"

Izzy sat up straighter on the cushions. "What did she say? Is something wrong?"

Seth looked between them, then rubbed a hand down his face again. "She wants us to email over the screenshots. All of them: the messages, the videos, usernames, everything. Says she'll pass it to digital harm."

"So, they're taking it seriously?" Natalia asked.

"Sort of," he muttered. "Hard to tell with her. She sounded more like we were bothering her than raising something important."

Izzy huffed. "That tracks."

Natalia crossed her arms. "And Jonah?"

Seth hesitated a moment. "He's being released. Later this afternoon."

Izzy's eyes snapped wide. "What? Really? Why didn't you lead with that?"

Natalia blinked. "Released how?"

"On bail," Seth said. "McIntyre wouldn't go into detail. Said the paperwork would be at the gate when we collect him. Told us to expect a call from Wetherby once he's cleared for pickup."

"That's it?" Natalia asked, stunned. "Just like that?"

Seth's mouth twisted. "Not 'just like that'. She made it very clear Jonah's not off any hook. Said she's 'retaining investigative control'- whatever that means. She's keeping something back. I could hear it in her voice."

Izzy frowned. "So, he's getting out, but they're still watching him."

Seth nodded. "And probably watching us too. They have something, they must have..."

The room fell quiet.

Natalia moved back toward the table and sank into a chair. "So, you think they know something we don't?"

Seth didn't answer.

He already knew they did.

And he had a feeling they would find out what. Sooner rather than later.

Chapter Thirty-Six

Friday, 28th March 2025 – 15:52

Wetherby Young Offenders' Institution – Processing and Release

The knock came at the door just after half-past three.
Jonah sat up stiffly on the edge of his mattress, unsure whether he'd been dozing or just staring at the floor long enough for time to dissolve. The officer outside didn't wait.
"Overaugh," came the voice, clear but without urgency. "Get your things. You're being discharged."
Discharged.

It didn't feel like the word should apply to him.
He stood, stiff from the cold mattress and a week of restless nights and reached for the folded sweatshirt and joggers he'd been issued on intake. They still smelled like disinfectant and cheap soap. Nothing here ever smelled like people.
The door buzzed open, and he stepped into the corridor. A

different officer was waiting this time; one he hadn't seen before. Stockier. More tired looking. He didn't smile.
"Follow me."
They walked in silence through a series of long, undistinguished hallways, every corner feeling like it could just as easily turn into another week.
At the processing unit, Jonah was handed over to a younger officer, this one holding a clipboard and wearing thin latex gloves.
"Stand there. State your full name."
"Jonah Thomas Overaugh."
"Date of birth?"
"Twelfth November 2006."
The officer checked a few boxes, then turned and opened a narrow metal locker along the wall. Inside was a sealed evidence bag. His clothes, folded into a clear plastic pouch. His hoodie. His jeans. His phone and wallet were in separate smaller bags; each tagged with the date of intake.
"You'll change into your original clothing. Anything issued here stays. If you want to take the soap or toothpaste, be my guest."
Jonah nodded numbly and stepped into the adjacent cubicle to change. The clothes felt wrong... stiff, foreign... like he was climbing back into the skin of someone who didn't quite exist anymore.

When he emerged, the officer handed him a manila envelope. "These are your bail conditions. Read them before you sign the release sheet."

Jonah opened the flap. Inside were three typed pages outlining his temporary freedom. A mix of legal formality and looming consequence.

- Remain at Moorside House, Accrington.
- Do not contact Brendan Hughes or any family member either directly or indirectly.
- Surrender passport to East Lancashire CID by Monday.
- Attend any future court appearances or interviews when summoned.
- Do not delete or alter any digital communications or records.
- You may be recalled to custody if you breach any of these terms.

He signed where they pointed.
The final step was retrieving his phone, battery dead, and wallet, which felt absurdly light in his hand. No charger. No receipts. No cash.
"Alright," the officer said, stepping back and opening the outer gate. "That's it. You're free to go."
Free.
Jonah stepped outside and squinted against the afternoon light. It wasn't even sunny, just pale and damp and too open. The air smelled of diesel and cut grass. A van pulled away in the distance.
And there, parked crookedly near the edge of the visitors' bay, was his dad's car.
Seth was leaning against the bonnet, coat collar turned up,

arms folded, eyes already on him.

For a moment, neither of them moved.

Then Jonah crossed the car park slowly, each step carrying a weight he couldn't quite identify. He stopped a few feet from his father; hands jammed into his hoodie pockets.

Seth gave a small nod.

"Alright, son?"

Jonah nodded once. "Yeah."

Then they hugged, All the animosity and lies forgotten in that instant, Jonah was still Seth's son and Jonah felt lucky to have a dad like him.

Seth reached for the passenger door. "Come on. Let's go home."

The car hummed quietly as Seth merged onto the motorway, windscreen wipers squeaking across a light drizzle. Neither of them spoke for a few miles. The tension between them wasn't hostile; just full of the heaviness that you can't hold in your hands.

Jonah sat hunched in the passenger seat, flipping through the bail papers again. The edges were already creased. He stared at the top condition for the third time.

"'Do not contact Brendan Hughes or any family member either directly or indirectly,'" he read aloud, voice low. "So... they don't think he's dead."

Seth kept his eyes on the road. "Doesn't sound like it.

"They wouldn't write it that way if they knew."

Seth gave a tight nod. "They'd say something like 'Do not discuss the ongoing investigation' or 'Do not make statements relating to the incident'."

Jonah exhaled through his nose, then glanced sideways. "Either they haven't found anything or they're waiting to see what we do next."

Seth tapped the steering wheel with his thumb. "That's what I was thinking. Could be a fishing expedition."

"Yeah," Jonah said, eyes narrowing. "Set the bail terms. Watch who I talk to. Who we talk to."

Seth's jaw flexed. "The wording's deliberate. They're keeping us in the dark for a reason."

"You think they're bugging the house?"

Seth shook his head. "Too risky. And illegal without a warrant. They'd need more than a hunch for that."

"Maybe they're watching from a distance. Monitoring socials. Checking who we meet."

"They'd be idiots not to."

Jonah slumped deeper into the seat, the bail papers crumpling in his hands. "So, we're not out of this."

"No," Seth said flatly. "We're not. You're out of the cell. That's all and for now, that's enough."

They drove on in silence for a few moments, the motorway stretching ahead, grey and relentless.

Jonah eventually asked, "So what do we do?"

Seth glanced at him. "We keep quiet. We stay alert. We don't assume anything. And most importantly... we don't panic."

Chapter Thirty-Seven

Friday, 28th March 2025 – 19:24

Moorside House – Driveway

Jonah stared up at Moorside through the passenger window, chest tightening. It looked the same. Still. Cold. But something had shifted. He wasn't just coming home.
He was returning, changed.
The front door opened before the engine cut out.
Natalia stood just beyond the threshold; arms folded. She didn't move until Jonah stepped out of the car, backpack slung over one shoulder like a schoolboy caught smoking.
Then she crossed the gravel and wrapped her arms around him.
No tears. Just contact. Solid and silent.
Izzy hovered behind her, eyes red but dry, her posture taut.
Seth shut the car door with a little too much force and rounded the bonnet slowly.
They entered the house together, closing the door behind

them like a vault sealing shut.

Inside, the hallway smelled faintly of furniture polish and lavender reed diffusers. Too normal. Too clean. But definitely no bleach.

They made their way to the snug, the only room that had started to feel lived-in again. Lydia gave a single bark from the top of the stairs and came piling down.

Jonah sat on the edge of the low sofa. Natalia perched beside him. Izzy curled into the floor cushions as usual, arms around her knees. Seth remained standing, arms crossed, his silhouette dark against the window light.

For a moment, no one spoke.

Then Seth cleared his throat. "We need to talk about next steps."

Jonah gave a quiet laugh. "Thought we were done with steps. Turns out, it's just stairs into more shit."

"No jokes," Seth said. "Not now."

Izzy leant into Jonah's ear "Apparently it's still too soon."

Natalia scolded at Izzy and then nodded at Seth. "He's right. We need to be careful. Everything we say, everything we do. The bail conditions are clear."

"They're watching," Izzy said.

"Probably," Seth replied. "Not inside the house, not legally, we're not an organised crime group. But they'll be monitoring movement, social media, who we contact. They're waiting for something to slip."

Jonah leaned forward, elbows on knees. "Then we don't slip."

Seth nodded. "Exactly. No texts. No speculation. No whispered theories. Not in the car. Not in the garden. Not

online. If you don't need to say it: don't."
Then Jonah said: "We don't react. Not until we know, or at least have an idea on what the police have"
Seth met his son's gaze. "And if they interview you again? Which I'm sure they will."
Jonah looked at him steadily. "I stick to what I've already said. Which was very little in the first place."
Seth nodded slowly. "Then we hold the line."
The rest of the night passed in quiet company.
No one said much. The television flickered in the corner of the snug, playing something none of them were watching. A half-eaten takeaway sat cooling on the table. Lydia lay curled by the hearth, sensing the shift in the air but wisely keeping to herself.
They didn't speak about Brendan.
Or the police.
Or the statue.
It was enough, for now, just to be in the same room. To breathe the same air. To exist together without the weight of questions pulling them apart.
At one point, Izzy raised her eyebrows and leaned toward Jonah, breaking the silence with a sharp grin.
"So, come on then," she said, tone faux light. "Any bigger boys try and make you their prison wife, or what?"
Jonah snorted. "No."
Izzy's face fell into mock disappointment. "Seriously? Not even a toothbrush shiv or a bunkmate named Kev with a tattoo of his ex on his neck?"
"No Kevs. No shivs. Just a lot of silence and rubber

mattresses," Jonah replied.

She leaned back with a small huff. "Ugh. That's so boring."

Natalia gave her a look, but Izzy just shrugged. "I'm allowed to find trauma funny. It's how I keep mine in perspective."

Seth, for once, didn't argue.

When the clock crept past ten, they moved almost in unison. No discussion. No nod of agreement. Just a quiet, collective rise.

Jonah headed up the stairs first, Lydia padding behind him. Natalia turned off the lamp. Seth locked the door. Izzy lingered, then followed her parents without a word, though not without muttering something under her breath about "a wasted opportunity for gritty institutional folklore."

They went to bed at nearly the same time. Not because they were tired, but because there was nothing else left to do.

And for the first time in what felt like forever, Moorside held them gently.

Unspoken. Fragile.

Together.

For now.

The dream did not come fast.

Once again it crept. Folding them in. One by one.

It didn't slip through the cracks of sleep or creep around the edges.

It took them.

One moment, they were in their own rooms - beds creaking, the house settling, sleep just beginning. The next, they were standing together, all four of them - Seth, Natalia, Izzy, and Jonah - side by side in the moonlit field beneath the black sky.

The grass was tall, wet with dew, and cold against their bare feet.

They didn't question it. They didn't speak.

They all knew.

They were back.

Moorside House loomed behind them, hunched and skeletal. Its windows were dark. Its stones wet. Its chimneys crooked like broken fingers. The air buzzed; not with sound, but with presence.

Jonah looked down at his hands, felt the grain of the earth between his toes. "This is different," he said.

"We're here together again," Natalia whispered.

Izzy was staring at the trees. "We're not watching this time," she said. "We're inside it."

Then the wind shifted.

And they all turned.

From the trees, the little girl burst into view. White nightgown, blonde hair wild in the wind. She ran with the frantic, full-bodied terror of someone who already knew no one was coming to help.

"Lottie," Natalia breathed.

The name didn't echo - it was swallowed by the field.

They didn't move. They couldn't. Their bodies were locked in place, hearts pounding as the girl tore past them, her tiny feet making no sound in the grass.

Then...

Bang.

The green front door of Moorside House flew open with a violent slam.

The woman burst out - no more than thirty - frantic and breathless, one shoe barely on, her coat half-buttoned. Her chestnut hair pinned in 1940s victory rolls, coming loose as she ran onto the drive.

"LOTTIE!" she screamed.

Her voice wasn't theatrical. It was real. Raw. The sound of something breaking.

"Lottie, come back!"

She stumbled down the steps, scanning the horizon, eyes wide and wet. Behind her, the house loomed silently, and to its left, the olive-green van coughed out a sick breath of smoke. Its back doors hung open. Waiting.

The Overaughs all turned at once as a second figure appeared... the matron.

Stout, grey-dressed, with hard shoes and harder posture, she moved with rigid urgency. Her hands gripped the bannister. Her voice was not cruel, but neither was it kind.

"Mrs Hawthorn!" she called. "Please, come back inside."

The young mother ignored her, already running across the driveway.

Seth whispered once again, "She can't see her."

"She doesn't know," Seth said. "The girl's gone too far. Too low. The ha-ha blocks her. She can't see below the rise."

The others followed his gaze.

Below the slope, just beyond the ditch... the figure was there. Long coat. Wide-brimmed hat. Movements slow, certain,

terrifying.
He had waited for the blind spot like he always did.
They saw the girl falter. Stumble.
And then, in a blur of motion, he was on her.
His arms closed around her, and she vanished beneath the grass.
There was no scream.
Just a soundless collapse, like breath being snuffed from the world.
Seth's voice broke through again, barely above a whisper. "She never saw it. She never saw her taken."
The others stared... at the woman crying out in the field, at the van, at the motionless figure rising slowly from the grass.
And then - as always - he turned.
Toward them.
His head tilted. Slowly. Deliberately.
Jonah stepped back.
Izzy whimpered.
Natalia's breath caught.
The man's coat began to fold inward again, as if devoured by shadow. His shape warped, his body narrowing, smoke pouring upward from his limbs.
And beneath it all, his face began to show.
Not fully.
Just flashes.
Flesh like bruised parchment. Jaw tight. Stubble-lined mouth curled into something close to a smile... but empty, corrupted.
His eyes were dark hollows.

And still... still... they saw a reflection of something human.
Something horribly, inescapably familiar.
Seth.
But not him.
A version rotted from the inside out. Worn like a costume by something that wanted to wear a man's skin and still didn't quite understand how.
And then; beside him, rising from the edge of the house...
The statue.
Black basalt. Hooded. Still.
Watching.
But no longer passive.
It was breathing.
Its chest rose and fell with the rhythm of the dream. Its arms shifted just enough to suggest awareness.
And then...
Its eyes opened.
Two gaping, lightless voids, as though someone had scooped the soul out of stone.
And the voice came.
Not spoken.
Felt.
Felt through the marrow of their bones. Felt in the twitch behind their eyes.
"You're mine now."
And in that moment the Overaughs' awoke in unison
Each bedroom light went on in turn and they all marched down to the kitchen for the inevitable dream debriefing.
No one had called the others down. No doors knocked. No

words exchanged. But somehow, they all ended up in the same place; barefoot, pale, and silent... like sleepwalkers pulled by the same current.

Jonah sat with his hands wrapped around an empty mug. Natalia was on autopilot pouring boiling water over a solitary teabag. Izzy had her head resting on the kitchen table, eyes open, staring at the grain of the wood like it might offer an explanation.

Seth stood with both hands on the back of his chair, not yet sitting.

It was Jonah who spoke first.

"We were all there again"

Natalia nodded slowly. "Together."

"It wasn't just similar," Izzy murmured, voice muffled by her sleeve. "It was identical. I saw you three standing next to me. I felt you there."

Seth finally lowered himself into the chair. "We saw the same thing. The same girl. The same field. The same... man."

Jonah looked between them. "So, it's real then."

Seth gave a tight nod. "As real as it gets in dreams."

"But it's not just a dream," Natalia said. "Not anymore. We weren't witnessing it. We were part of it. The way the wind felt. The weight in my chest. I could feel the wet grass against my legs."

Izzy rubbed her arms. "And the sound. Did anyone else notice that? How quiet it got when he grabbed her? Like the air itself was holding its breath."

"The ha-ha," Seth said suddenly. "It's always there. That damned ditch. I explained it in the dream, didn't I?"

Jonah nodded. "Yeah. You said the mother couldn't see Lottie being taken because of the slope. The man knew the blind spot."

Natalia swallowed. "And she just kept shouting; over and over. But Lottie was already gone."

They fell silent, the only sound the subtle hiss of the kettle long forgotten on the side.

Seth exhaled. "We saw her taken. Again."

"And this time," Izzy added, sitting up straighter, "we saw him."

Jonah looked over. "The man."

"The thing," she corrected. "Wearing dad's face."

"I didn't feel like him," Seth said quietly. "I wasn't in his skin this time. But I still knew... that version of me, it's like it was carved out of something else and left behind."

Natalia's fingers drummed on the mug. "And the statue?"

They all looked at each other.

"It was watching," Jonah said. "Breathing. Bigger."

"Its eyes opened," Natalia whispered. "Black holes. Like... like it absorbed the whole dream."

"And then it said it again," Izzy added. "'You're mine now'."

Seth's voice was hoarse. "So, what the hell does that mean?"

They all stared at the table.

No one had an answer.

Just the same word cycling silently through their heads.

Lottie.

And the sense that whatever had begun with Brendan, and bled into Jonah's lie, had reached back further than they could imagine. And it wasn't done with them yet.

Chapter Thirty-Eight

Saturday, 29th March 2025 – 09:54

"DAAAAAD!"
Izzy's scream tore through the house like a fire alarm. Not angry. Not playful. Urgent.
Seth dropped the box of cereal he'd just retrieved from the pantry and was already halfway down the hallway before Natalia had even stood up. Jonah bounded in from the snug, barefoot and wide-eyed.
Izzy was standing in the middle of the kitchen; phone held in front of her like it might explode.
"What is it?" Seth demanded. "Izzy?"
Her thumb was hovering over the screen, her voice sharp and breathless. "I think someone's trying to send a message. Not one of the hate ones. It's different. It just came in. Snapchat. A blue snap. Not a memory or video... just text. No Bitmoji. No location. The name's weird. Firepit Antics."
Jonah blinked. "What?"
Natalia moved beside her, peering over her shoulder. "Are you

sure it's not someone trolling again?"

"No," Izzy snapped. "It's not like the others. It's buried under loads of hate messages, yeah, but this one's clean. No streaks, no emoji spam, no threats. And it's not someone I know... look."

She tapped the ghost icon on the top left. No map. No username metadata. No emojis. Just the grey outline and the name: **Firepit Antics.**

"Random handle. No Bitmoji. No location permissions. Looks like a burner account," Jonah said.

"And it's a blue snap," Izzy added. "That means it's just a chat message, not a picture or a story. I opened it by accident while trying to block the last guy who told me I looked like I 'cover for murder in eyeliner'."

They all leaned closer as Izzy read the message aloud:

"Tell your brother that he went wild camping on the canal with a tent and swore him to secrecy, he wanted to be alone to clear his head."

She stared at it for a second. "It literally just arrived. Like less than a minute ago."

Jonah stepped forward. "Wait, what?"

Seth's eyes narrowed. "Is that what Jane would have said to the police."

Natalia stiffened. "No, why would she? Who would send it? And 'Firepit Antics'. That's a little too close to home don't you think"

"Someone's coaching a cover story," Seth murmured.

And just then... right before their eyes.... the text vanished. The snap blinked out, and the thread reset to empty. Then,

with a flicker, the contact disappeared entirely from Izzy's list.
"Gone." she breathed. "They deleted the account."
Jonah stared at her phone. "That means no return message. No callback. No trace unless Snapchat keeps server-side logs."
"They do," Seth said quickly. "But only for a very limited time. And even then, it's encrypted."
Izzy was already taking screenshots of the empty thread, the handle, and her contact screen.
"It's nothing," she muttered. "I mean... it's everything. But there's nothing left."
Seth reached for her phone. "Send me all those screenshots. I'll timestamp them and get them into a secure folder."
Natalia sat down heavily at the kitchen table. "So, whoever that was... they know we need a cover story, and they know something about the fire pit."
"They knew to send it through Izzy," Jonah added. "And to say I'd been sworn to secrecy."
"Which makes it seem premeditated," Seth finished grimly.
"This just seems to get stranger and stranger"
The kettle clicked off behind them. No one moved.
In the silence, Izzy whispered what they were all thinking:
"Someone out there is pulling strings. Why this message? Why now?"

Chapter Thirty-Nine

Saturday, 29th March 2025 – 10:14

Izzy had gone quiet.
Too quiet.
She sat cross-legged on the floor of the snug, her phone in her lap, mouth slightly open. The sound from the muted telly flickered in the background, but she didn't hear it. Not properly.
A minute passed before she said anything.
"Guys..."
No one responded. Seth was upstairs shaving. Natalia was in the laundry room. Jonah was slumped sideways on the arm of the sofa, scrolling through nothing.
Izzy said it again. Louder.
"GUYS!"
This time, her tone cut through the house like a sharp blade. Natalia was the first to appear, drying her hands with a tea towel. "What now, what is it?"
Izzy turned her phone toward her. "You need to get dad and

Jonah, I think I know why we got that message, It's on the Gazette Live site. Just went up three minutes ago."

Jonah leaned over from the sofa.

At the top of the screen was a headline in bold: 'BREAKING: Missing Teen Brendan Hughes Returns Home Safe'

'There is nothing further to report at this time as the police investigation is ongoing.'

Beneath it, a photo:

Brendan. Unmistakably him, standing just outside his mum's front door.

His hoodie was zipped halfway. His face looked paler than usual, gaunt but it was him. And Jane was beside him, one arm lightly around his back, her other hand shielding her eyes from the camera flash.

Natalia covered her mouth.

Jonah sat upright, like the wind had been knocked out of him by an enormous punch of relief. "He's back."

"They knew," Izzy said, almost to herself. "McIntyre knew yesterday, she must have. When you called."

"She didn't tell us," Natalia whispered. "She kept it quiet on purpose."

Jonah stood now. "Of course she did. It's strategy. Keep us in the dark, let us say or do something that contradicts what Brendan's going to tell them."

Seth appeared in the doorway, towel around his neck. "What's going on?"

Izzy held up the phone again, her voice clipped. "Your best mate, the not-so-headless watch-robber Brendan. Turns out he's not dead after all."

Seth took the phone and read in silence.
Jonah shook his head, pacing. "And now they're going to think I really knew. That I helped him vanish. That I was part of the story."
"They already do," Seth said grimly. "That's what this has all been about. The way McIntyre danced around it, the way that bail condition was written. She wanted to watch us sweat. And that snap message, clearly a tip off."
Natalia was still staring at the photo. "He looks... off."
"He is off," Izzy said. "He's a lying, thieving little toe rag."
"Or covering for someone, or something" Jonah added.
Seth handed the phone back. "They've staged this to end public speculation, but they've said nothing new. 'No further comment while the investigation is ongoing.' That means they've still got their claws in this."
Izzy suddenly blinked like she remembered something. "The Snapchat message. That was the prep. The warning. Firepit Antics was laying the groundwork."
"And now we're the ones holding the questions," Jonah said. "While Brendan's out there, smiling for the cameras like he's just come back from a school trip."
Natalia sat down slowly. "So, what happens now?"
Seth looked at all three of them.
"Now?" he said. "Now we assume we're being watched more than ever. And we don't give them a single thing they don't already know."
And for a long time, no-one spoke.
Seth broke the silence first.
"You should be rehearsing your story."

Jonah looked up, caught off-guard. "What?"

"I mean it," Seth said, his voice low but clipped. "Now that he's back... now that he's done his little smiling-for-the-papers routine... they'll be coming for you again. Probably Monday. Maybe sooner. They'll want to know exactly what you knew, when you knew it, and if you're still lying."

"I already told them," Jonah muttered, rubbing his thumb across a patch of worn wood on the bench. "Garage. Switch. Fell asleep. Left in the morning."

Seth shook his head. "No. That won't do anymore. Brendan's clearly told them he went camping and that you knew. That you 'swore to keep it quiet.' So, your 'asleep on the sofa' routine? That's gone. Dead in the water."

Jonah stared at the floor. "So... what, I just confess to helping him disappear? That sounds worse."

"No," Seth said firmly. "You don't confess. You adjust. You take control of your own story before someone else starts filling in the blanks."

Jonah's brow furrowed. "What does that even mean?"

"It means," Seth said, stepping forward, "you retract the parts that don't work. You say Brendan asked you to lie. You say you panicked. You say you waited with him while he packed his gear and then watched him walk off down the canal path. You were worried about him but didn't want to break his trust."

Jonah looked at him sceptically. "And that's better?"

"It's believable," Seth snapped. "It aligns you with what he's already probably said. You didn't 'help' him disappear; you covered for a friend who wanted space. You regretted it. You

were stupid. But you weren't criminal."
Jonah exhaled hard through his nose. "So, I just... change my statement?"
"You revise it," Seth said. "You say that in the confusion and fear of the police showing up, you panicked and simplified the truth. Now that Brendan is safe, you want to clarify. Nothing more."
Jonah ran both his hands through his hair, pacing the snug floor in three uneven steps. "What if they catch the timing? What if they say I had too much time to plan this with him?"
Seth didn't hesitate. "Then you lean into the guilt. You say you were scared. You say you didn't want Brendan to get into trouble, but when you saw what it was doing to your family, you knew you had to fix it."
Jonah turned sharply. "You sound like you've done this before."
"I've read a lot of statements," Seth replied. "And I've seen what happens to people who can't keep theirs straight."
Jonah was quiet for a long moment. Then, reluctantly, he spoke.
"So... the revised version is this: Brendan told me he was going wild camping to get his head straight as he was feeling very depressed. He asked me not to tell anyone, made me swear. I waited with him at the industrial estate, we talked, he packed a bag, and then I watched him head down the canal path alone and took his car home."
Seth nodded. "Exactly that. And when you got home, you tried to act normal. But when the police showed up, you panicked and gave them the version that sounded safest."

Jonah gave a dry laugh. "So, I'm still a liar. Just a different kind."

Seth held his gaze. "You're a survivor. There's a difference."

Jonah didn't respond.

But he started repeating the words anyway. Not because he believed them yet... but because he knew he'd have to.

Chapter Forty

Monday, 31st March 2025 – 09:09

Moorside House – Kitchen

The phone rang while the kettle was still warming.
Seth picked it up mid-boil, recognising the name on the screen with a grim sigh. He answered without enthusiasm.
"Mr Overaugh," came the solicitor's voice; nasal, clipped, and still somehow bored, even at just past seven. "As anticipated, the police would like to conduct a second interview with your son. Today."
Seth rubbed his forehead. "Right. What time?"
"You're expected at the station by 10:30am. Sharp. Jonah should bring the bail conditions paperwork with him. They'll want to review the terms before proceeding."
"And you'll be there?"
"I'll meet you outside. Don't be late… they've made it very clear this is a voluntary interview, but any sign of non-cooperation and they'll escalate."

Seth gritted his teeth. "Anything else?"

"Yes," the solicitor said. "Keep him quiet. No improvising, no speculation. If he's going to alter or 'clarify' his previous statement, now's the time to land it cleanly."

Seth hung up without saying goodbye.

He turned to find Jonah already at the table, halfway through a slice of toast, staring at him.

"Let me guess," Jonah said. "We've got somewhere to be."

"10:30," Seth replied, pouring the boiling water into his mug. "Time to rehearse your best version of the truth."

Monday, 31st March 2025 – 10:24

East Lancashire Police Station – Custody Suite

The reception smelt of overbrewed coffee and stale paperwork. Jonah stood between his father and the solicitor, hands in his pockets, hood down, trying to look neutral. Bored, even. Inside, he felt like glassware.

A uniformed officer stood behind a plexiglass screen, clipboard in hand.

"Name?"

"Jonah Overaugh."

"Here for re-interview. Voluntary, under caution. One solicitor present, Mr-?"

"Cartwright," the solicitor grunted, barely looking up from his phone.

The officer tapped at a keyboard. "Room Three. Take a seat in the waiting area, someone will come get you in a minute."

Jonah nodded, then followed Cartwright and Seth toward the plastic chairs against the wall. Natalia had stayed home; the family had agreed it was better that way. Less presence. Less pressure.

Within two minutes, the door buzzed open.

DC McIntyre entered, flanked by a different officer; male, broad-chested, unfamiliar. She looked the same as always: composed, alert, and completely unimpressed.

"Jonah," she said with a polite nod. "Thanks for coming in."

He stood.

"Come on through."

They walked down a short corridor to Interview Room Three. It was empty except for a rectangular table, four chairs, and a black wall-mounted recorder blinking silently in the corner. Jonah took the seat across from McIntyre.

The male officer remained standing by the door. Cartwright sat next to Jonah with the air of someone already inconvenienced.

McIntyre pressed a button on the digital unit.

"This is Detective Constable Sarah McIntyre," she said clearly. "Interview commencing at 10:31am, East Lancashire CID. Also present are DC Alston, Jonah Overaugh, and his legal representative Mr Cartwright. Jonah is here voluntarily. This interview is being conducted under caution."

She turned to Jonah.

"You are not under arrest, but you are under caution. That means you do not have to say anything. But it may harm your defence if you do not mention something now which you later rely on in court. Do you understand?"

Jonah nodded.

"Please answer verbally for the recording."

"Yes."

McIntyre folded her hands.

"Right. Let's go back to the beginning... Friday, March 14th. You've previously stated you were with Brendan Hughes, at his garage, playing video games until the early hours, before returning home. Do you stand by that version of events?"

Jonah glanced briefly at Cartwright, who didn't even look up. Then he drew a breath.

"I'd like to clarify my statement."

McIntyre blinked. Just once.

"Go on."

And the room fell completely still.

"I want to clarify parts of what I said in my first statement," he said, voice steady... rehearsed, but not robotic. "Not because I'm changing the truth, but because I panicked. I simplified things. It didn't feel safe to say more at the time."

McIntyre sat forward slightly. "Alright. Let's go through it."

Jonah nodded, swallowed, and began.

"I was with Brendan on the Friday night. But we weren't at his garage the whole time. We hung out there for a bit... played some games, talked. Then he told me he needed some time alone. Said he was going wild camping along the canal."

"Wild camping?" McIntyre echoed.

"Yeah," Jonah said. "He had his rucksack already packed. Tent, sleeping bag, all of it. I think he'd been planning it for a while."

"Did he say why?"

"He said he needed to clear his head. That he'd been feeling boxed in. That he didn't want anyone to bother him. He made me promise not to tell anyone."

"Swore you to secrecy?"

Jonah nodded. "Exactly. I know he'd been very down and low lately."

McIntyre leaned back slightly. "So, when did this conversation happen?"

Jonah thought for a second. "Maybe just after midnight. He was... calm. Kind of focused. Like he'd already made the decision."

"Where did you go after that?"

"We drove to the industrial estate; Moorside Industrial Estate. It's near the canal access. Brendan wanted to avoid street cameras, and that was the quietest way to get to the towpath without anyone seeing him."

"Was anyone else there?"

"No. Just us."

"Was he carrying anything unusual?"

"No weapons, if that's what you mean. Just the bag. So, whatever he had in the bag, I didn't see inside it."

McIntyre scribbled something in her notebook.

"So, you parked at the estate," she said. "Then what?"

"We sat in the car for a bit. Talked. I asked if he was sure. He said he'd done it before, just never told anyone. Said it helped him 'reset'."

McIntyre raised an eyebrow. "Did he specify where he was going?"

"Just along the canal. Heading toward Burnley. He said he'd

find a field or a clearing. Something away from dog walkers."
"And you let him go?"
Jonah nodded. "I asked if I should come with him. He said no. Said the whole point was to be alone. Then he got out of the car, put on his rucksack, and walked into the dark."
McIntyre paused, letting the silence stretch.
"Did you watch him leave?"
Jonah hesitated.
"Yes," he said. "He walked down the path. I stayed until I couldn't see him anymore."
"Then what?"
"I drove back to Brendan's house," Jonah said. "I told his mum he was sleeping in. Said I was heading off. Then I went home."
McIntyre nodded slowly, then flipped back a page in her notebook.
"So... your initial statement claimed you were at Brendan's garage all night. Playing Switch. Sleeping. You didn't mention the industrial estate. Or the canal. Or any of this."
Jonah looked her in the eye. "I know."
"Why lie?"
He sighed. "Because I didn't want to betray him. He made me promise. And I got scared; I really thought it would help him. I didn't want the police to think I'd helped him disappear."
McIntyre nodded thoughtfully. "So, you told a lie. To protect a friend."
"Yes."
"Which led to a missing persons inquiry. A forensic sweep of

Brendan's house. Your own arrest and remand. And hours of police time."

Jonah's throat tightened. "I didn't mean for any of that."

McIntyre tapped her pen against the edge of her notebook. "You understand how serious this is?"

"Yes."

"And yet you still chose to withhold information."

Jonah said nothing.

McIntyre studied him for a moment. "A couple more questions. Did Brendan ever talk about staging his own disappearance? Did he ever mention wanting people to think he was missing?"

"No," Jonah said quickly. "He just wanted to be left alone. That's all."

"Mm..."

"Have you ever seen Brendan take drugs?"

"err... No... Never"

"Interesting..."

McIntyre tapped the pen slowly against the desk, watching Jonah with the type of stare that made people squirm.

"You understand," she said coolly, "that lying to the police during a missing persons investigation is not a slap on the wrist, Jonah. It's not just 'being stupid' or 'protecting a friend.' It's a criminal offence. Wasting police time. Perverting the course of justice. You've seen a custody cell. You should know by now that we take those things seriously."

Jonah swallowed but said nothing.

She leaned forward slightly, not breaking eye contact.

"And while we're at it, let's talk about something else you

conveniently omitted."

She flipped a page in her notes, then looked up.

"You drove Brendan's car that night, didn't you?"

Jonah shifted uncomfortably. "Yes."

"You're eighteen and you don't hold a full licence. You weren't insured. That means you were driving illegally. That, too, is a criminal offence. Driving otherwise than in accordance with a licence, no insurance, possibly taking a vehicle without consent... Depending on what Brendan told us, any of those could land you right back where you started."

"I wasn't joyriding," Jonah said quietly. "It was just parked. We weren't going anywhere."

"Intent doesn't matter," McIntyre snapped. "It's the act. And it's all part of the bigger picture here, Jonah. You weren't just a bystander. You were actively misleading an investigation, operating a vehicle illegally, and covering for a disappearance that sparked public attention."

She paused, letting the words hang like smoke.

"You've got one chance to keep yourself on the right side of this. If there's anything else you've been holding back, now is the time."

Jonah met her eyes and said nothing.

She closed her notebook and sat back.

"Well, Jonah, thank you for clarifying. This interview will be added to the case file and reviewed by the CPS. You're still on bail. Your conditions remain unchanged for now."

Jonah blinked. "That's it?"

"For now," McIntyre said. "But I'd recommend you don't go far. This might not be the last time that we talk."

Chapter Forty-One

Monday, 31st March 2025 – 12:15

East Lancashire Police Station – Car Park

The door to the station burst open with a dull clatter of metal and frosted glass.

Jonah stormed out first, his trainers skidding slightly on the concrete ramp. He spotted Seth immediately, standing beside the car, eyes locked on the entrance like a man waiting for a verdict.

Jonah didn't slow until he reached him.

"She knows," he said, breathless. "Not everything, but enough. She hammered me on the driving, the lie, the missing hours. Asked if Brendan staged it. Said I wasted police time."

Seth's jaw clenched. "Did you stick to it?"

"Yeah. I ran the line. Canal. Tent. Swore me to secrecy. Didn't flinch." Jonah ran a hand down his face. "But she's watching. Hard. Like she's waiting for me to slip."

Behind them, Cartwright emerged at a more leisurely pace, flicking the clasp on his battered leather satchel. He gave Seth a brief nod, more out of formality than warmth.

"Well," he said with a sigh, "he didn't confess to anything stupid. That's progress. I'll wait to see what CPS says. Don't expect medals."

Then, without waiting for a reply, he turned and shuffled off across the car park, his shoes scuffing against the asphalt like punctuation marks.

Seth waited until he was out of earshot, then turned back to Jonah. "You alright?"

Jonah gave a hollow laugh. "Depends on what you mean by 'alright'."

Seth unlocked the car.

"Get in. Let's get you home. You're not in custody, so that's a massive win!"

Monday, 31st March 2025 – 12:46

Moorside House – Kitchen

The kitchen was quiet when they walked in; too quiet. Natalia sat at the table; Izzy was perched on the window ledge.

They both looked up the second the door opened.

"Well?" Natalia asked, already rising from her chair. "How bad was it?"

Jonah shrugged off his coat, slinging it over the back of the nearest chair. "She went in hard. Told me I wasted police time. Brought up the car. Said driving without a licence was a separate offence."

Izzy winced. "Ouch."

"She's not wrong," Seth added, closing the door behind him. "But she was clearly fishing. Pressured him on whether Brendan staged the whole thing. Whether Jonah helped. Whether he was lying to protect someone."

"I stuck to the story," Jonah said, pacing a slow line from the table to the sink. "Said Brendan told me he was going wild camping. Swore me to secrecy. I admitted I was scared when he didn't come back and that I panicked. That's why I gave the first version."

Natalia exchanged a look with Seth. "Did she believe you?"

Jonah shook his head. "I don't know. She didn't say much. Just scribbled in her notebook and stared at me like she was waiting for a crack."

"She said CPS would review the statement," Seth added. "Didn't give a timeline. Just reminded us that he's still on bail."

Izzy slid off the ledge and leaned on the counter beside Jonah. "So... we're still in hot water?"

"Yes," Jonah replied. "The water's just a little cooler now."

Natalia sat back down, visibly trying to think through the implications. "So, what happens next?"

"We stay alert," Seth said. "They've had their second go. That means their next move will either be charging... or waiting for us to screw up."

Izzy frowned. "Or both."

The wind rattled faintly against the windowpanes. No one

said anything for a few moments.

Then Jonah spoke again.

"She asked if Brendan talked about staging it. Disappearing. Like she already knows he did and she asked if I'd ever seen him taking drugs."

Seth looked at Natalia. "So, it begins. We have way too many unknowns and uncontrollable elements for my liking. I don't think time is our friend right now."

Natalia didn't answer straight away.

She was staring at the far wall; not at anything in particular, just fixed on a patch of air above the radiator like it might blink and reveal something. She blinked once, slowly, and then turned to the others.

Her voice was quiet. But steady.

Almost detached.

"If Brendan's alive…"

She looked at Jonah.

"…and we didn't kill him…"

She looked at Izzy.

Finally, she looked at Seth, who stared back, suddenly very still.

"…then who did we kill?"

Epilogue

Friday, 14th March 2025 – 20:41

Carmel-by-the-Sea, California

The nurses dimmed the lights in Room 214.
Meredith Richardson (nee Hawthorn) sat on the edge of the bed, the same way she had every Friday evening for as long as she could remember. Her hair was neatly brushed; silver waves gathered over one shoulder. Her robe was soft, cotton, pale lavender. On her lap, folded with delicate precision, was a well-worn shawl that had once belonged to her mother.
Outside, the wind moved through the pine trees and coastal fog crept across the window. From her vantage point, she could just see the moon; fractured through the top corner of the blinds. It was always clearer on Fridays, as if it knew.
She reached for the amber bottle on the tray beside her. Two small pills – one for sleep, one for blood pressure. She placed them on her tongue and swallowed them dry.

No need for water.

The dream would come either way.

They used to call it hysteria, back when she was twelve and first started talking about it. They said it was linked to "women's troubles" based on her age and family history.

Then it became traumatic grief syndrome in the fifties, and night terror recall in the seventies.

Later, a Harvard-trained doctor labelled it persistent episodic intrusion.

By the time she was eighty, her latest neurologist gave it a newer name: intergenerational trauma imprint, spoken like he'd just discovered it himself.

None of them were wrong. But none of them understood.

Meredith didn't believe she was sick, she knew she was remembering.

And remembering was its own kind of curse. Especially when they are not your memories to begin with.

"Are you ready, sweetheart?" a voice asked gently from the door.

It was Emma tonight, the night nurse with the soft hands. Meredith liked Emma, she was kind and sweet.

Meredith smiled faintly. "As I'll ever be."

The covers were pulled back. Her slippers removed. She lay down slowly, bones creaking like old floorboards. Emma helped guide her legs under the quilt, then fluffed the pillow behind her head.

"Good dreams tonight," Emma whispered, reaching for the lamp.

Meredith almost laughed.
"It will be the same one as always" she said softly. "Always on a Friday."
Emma didn't reply. She'd heard that line before.
The light clicked off.
Meredith stared at the ceiling for a long moment, letting the silence wrap around her like the quilts of Moorside once had. Her breathing slowed. Her fingers curled slightly against the edge of the sheet. She had learnt long ago that trying to avoid it was inevitable and the quicker it came, the quicker it was gone.
She could already feel the grass under her feet.
She could smell the orchard.
Hear the wind through the willow tree that hadn't existed in decades.
It was always the same dream, Always Hannibal sobbing, Always Elias frantic, Always Lydia defiant.
She was 91 years old.
She had lived through wars, continents, heartbreak and wonder.
But every Friday night, as sleep took hold, she was back in Moorside for the same grizzly vision.

Saturday, 15th March 2025 – 07:15

Carmel-by-the-Sea, California

The blinds were already cracked when the door opened softly.
"Good morning, Meredith," Emma said, her tone light.

"Slept in today, hmm?"

She moved gently around the bed, tray in hand, expecting the usual murmured response and polite half-smile from her residents usually tortured sleep. But Meredith wasn't curled under the quilt, eyes fluttering awake as she always was. She was already sitting bolt upright, hands gripping the sheet, her face pale and slack with disbelief.

Emma paused. "Are you alright?"

Meredith blinked hard. "What time is it?"

"Quarter past seven," Emma replied. "You're usually up by six, but you were sleeping so soundly I left you alone."

"I didn't dream," Meredith snapped, her voice sharp enough to startle them both. Her hands fumbled toward the edge of the bed. "I didn't have the dream. I always have the dream."

Emma set the tray down. "That's not necessarily a bad thing, is it?"

"You don't understand," Meredith said, already swinging her legs over the edge of the bed. "It's never not happened. Every Friday. Since I was eight. And last night..."

She broke off, shaking her head as if trying to force the memory loose. But there was nothing. Just blankness. Quiet. Restful. Horrible quiet.

"No orchard. No grass. No wind. No Hannibal. No statue. Nothing." She looked up, eyes wide.

Emma moved toward her cautiously. "Let's get you dressed and have some breakfast, okay? Maybe it was just a fluke. Sleep cycles change."

"I need to speak to my daughter," Meredith said, ignoring her. Her voice was firmer now, laced with something almost

childlike. "Call her. Please. Now."
Emma hesitated.
"Call my daughter," Meredith said again, more forcefully.

"Something's changed."

Reading Group Guide

Moorside House: The Series of Silence – Book 1

Thank you for choosing to read The Silence We Hide. This is the first step into the world of Moorside House: The Series of Silence, and while many questions linger - and many more answers are still to come in the series - we hope this book has already sparked reflection and debate. For now, as you gather with your reading group, below are some discussion points to explore the choices, themes, and moral complexities faced by the Overaugh family.

This guide is designed to help you explore the themes, characters, and questions at the heart of The Silence We Hide.

Discussion Questions

Morality and Family: Seth and Natalia choose to cover up what happened rather than call the police. Do you believe they were protecting their family, or do you see their actions as indefensible? How far would you go to protect the people you love?

Truth and Silence: Silence shapes the Overaughs' lives in different ways - secrecy, denial, omission. Do you think silence is ever a form of protection, or is it always corrosive? Jonah and Brendan: Jonah sits in the car while Brendan enters Moorside, telling himself he isn't really involved. Is omission as culpable as action? How does his silence compare to his parents'?

Izzy's Role: Izzy witnesses her parents' decisions up close. How do you think this experience shapes her differently from Jonah? Did her reactions reflect innocence, morality or naivety? Should she have phoned the police?

The Statue and the House: Do you interpret the black basalt statue as a supernatural force, or a psychological projection of guilt and trauma? What does Moorside House itself symbolise for the family and is the house a different entity from the statue?

Generational Burden: The story suggests that the Overaughs are only the latest family to be haunted by events at Moorside. How do you think generational secrets shape the morality of the present?

Justice vs. Survival: Do you feel the Overaughs deserve exposure and punishment, or do you sympathise with their choice to survive? How do you weigh justice against family loyalty?

As you reflect on the Overaughs' choices, remember that this is only the beginning of Moorside's story. The shadows of the past run deep, and in the next book - The Silence We Share - new voices and old secrets will push the family further into moral grey zones where survival and truth collide. Thank you for reading and discussing this story; your insights bring the silence to life!

Coming next in Moorside House:
The Series of Silence

HEATH GROVES

THE SILENCE WE SHARE

THE HOUSE OF OVERAUGH
The Series of Silence · Book 2

DON'T BREAK THE SILENCE.
PRE-ORDER NOW

Silence doesn't keep the truth buried. As police pressure mounts and Moorside's dark history stirs to life, Jonah, Izzy, Seth, and Natalia discover that the past is not only alive, it is waiting. And the more they try to hide, the more the silence demands to be heard.

The following is an extract from Moorisde House: The Series of Silence Book 2: The Silence We Share.

He lingered on his name with mocking precision - "you are different. You are no innocent. You are corrupt, venal, violent. You are meat already spoiled, and to carve upon such meat is a greater delight altogether. I shall flay your soul until there is nothing left but rags. And then I shall begin anew, for there is no death here, only my hand, and my will, and your endless screams."

He stepped forward, his shadow spilling across the nothingness, crawling over his victim like oil. "I have an eternity to make an art of your undoing. You shall scream, and I shall savour. And when you think the end has come, when you believe yourself emptied, I shall begin again, and again, and again, until time itself has forgotten you."

He tried to speak, but no words came, only a strangled rasp. The void around him pulsed in time with his terror, the shadows dragging him down, deeper and deeper into his domain.

The figure tilted its head, studying him with grotesque delight. "You are mine now, resident in my dominion. And in it, you shall serve as my amusement, my canvas, my unending sport." The grin widened, teeth flashing like the edge of a blade.

"Welcome," the figure said, his voice dry as dust yet cutting through the gloom. "Welcome to the Dark Quarters."

"Now… let us get started."

THE SILENCE WE HIDE

THE HOUSE OF OVERAUGH